KEANE

ENFIELD LIBRARIES

9120000824483

MATT & TOM OLDFIELD

CLASSIC FOOTBALL HEROES

KEANE

FROM THE PLAYGROUND TO THE PITCH

DINO

First published by Dino Books in 2024,
an imprint of Bonnier Books UK,
4th Floor, Victoria House, Bloomsbury Square, London WC1B 4DA
Owned by Bonnier Books,
Sveavägen 56, Stockholm, Sweden

𝕏 @UFHbooks
𝕏 @footieheroesbks
www.heroesfootball.com
www.bonnierbooks.co.uk

Text © Matt Oldfield 2024

All rights reserved. No part of this publication may be reproduced, stored in a retrieval system, or transmitted in any form or by any means, without the prior permission in writing of the publisher, nor be otherwise circulated in any form of binding or cover other than that in which it is published and without a similar condition including this condition being imposed on the subsequent purchaser.

Paperback ISBN: 978 1 78946 790 1
E-book ISBN: 978 1 78946 797 0

British Library cataloguing-in-publication data:
A catalogue record for this book is available from the British Library.

Printed and bound in Great Britain by Clays Ltd, Elcograf S.p.A.

3 5 7 9 10 8 6 4 2

All names and trademarks are the property of their respective owners, which are in no way associated with Dino Books. Use of these names does not imply any cooperation or endorsement.

For Noah, Nico, Arlo and Lila

Matt Oldfield is a children's author focusing on the wonderful world of football. His other books include *Unbelievable Football* (winner of the 2020 Children's Sports Book of the Year) and the *Johnny Ball: Football Genius* series. In association with his writing, Matt also delivers writing workshops in schools.

Cover illustration by Dan Leydon.
To learn more about Dan, visit danleydon.com
To purchase his artwork visit etsy.com/shop/footynews
Or just follow him on X @danleydon

TABLE OF CONTENTS

ACKNOWLEDGEMENTS 9

CHAPTER 1 – 'WE'VE GOT OUR TROPHY BACK!' 11

CHAPTER 2 – A UNITED FAMILY 18

CHAPTER 3 – RISING WITH ROCKMOUNT 23

CHAPTER 4 – MIDFIELD MENACE 30

CHAPTER 5 – DUBLIN DESPAIR 35

CHAPTER 6 – TIME FOR PLAN B 41

CHAPTER 7 – THE BIG BREAKTHROUGH 46

CHAPTER 8 – A DAY OF SURPRISES 54

CHAPTER 9 – FOREST HIGHS AND LOWS 61

CHAPTER 10 – TRANSFER TWISTS 69

CHAPTER 11 – A DREAM START AT UNITED 74

CHAPTER 12 – **A WILD WORLD CUP: PART ONE** 82

CHAPTER 13 – **SECOND BEST** 89

CHAPTER 14 – **KEEPING UP WITH THE 'KIDS'** 95

CHAPTER 15 – **CAPTAIN KEANO AND A LOST SEASON** 103

CHAPTER 16 – **THE TREBLE** 108

CHAPTER 17 – **CRUISING** 116

CHAPTER 18 – **A WILD WORLD CUP: PART TWO** 124

CHAPTER 19 – **ON TOP OF THE MOUNTAIN AGAIN** 129

CHAPTER 20 – **A NEW ROLE** 134

CHAPTER 21 – **LEAVING UNITED, CHOOSING CELTIC** 140

CHAPTER 22 – **THE NEW BOSS** 145

CHAPTER 23 – **TELLING IT HOW IT IS** 152

KEANE HONOURS 166

GREATEST MOMENTS 169

TEST YOUR KNOWLEDGE 172

PLAY LIKE YOUR HEROES 174

ACKNOWLEDGEMENTS

First of all I'd like to thank everyone at Bonnier Books for supporting me and for running the ever-expanding UFH ship so smoothly. Writing stories for the next generation of football fans is both an honour and a pleasure. Thanks also to my agent, Nick Walters, for helping to keep my dream job going, year after year.

Next up, an extra big cheer for all the teachers, booksellers and librarians who have championed these books, and, of course, for the readers. The success of this series is truly down to you.

Okay, onto friends and family. I wouldn't be writing this series if it wasn't for my brother Tom. I owe him so much and I'm very grateful for his belief in me as an author. I'm also very grateful to the rest of my family, especially Mel, Noah, Nico, and of course Mum and Dad. To my parents, I owe my biggest passions: football and books. They're a real inspiration for everything I do.

CHAPTER 1

"WE'VE GOT OUR TROPHY BACK!"

11 May 2003, Goodison Park – Final Day of the Premier League Season

Roy Keane had seen it all during his Manchester United career, including his fair share of drama on the final day of the season.

Today was different, though. There was a relaxed mood as Roy and his teammates stepped off the team bus and walked towards the away dressing room at Goodison Park. United would be taking on Everton in a few hours, but the Premier League trophy was already theirs.

After a tense, thrilling title race, United had held off

Arsenal with a game to spare. This afternoon's season finale had once looked like a must-win game, but now it would be more of a celebration.

'Over the years, we've won the title on the final day and lost the title on the final day,' said Roy's teammate Ryan Giggs, or 'Giggsy' as they all called him. 'I've got to admit, it's nice not to have that pressure this year.'

Roy grinned, thinking back over the ten years of games that he and Giggsy had played together. 'Yeah, and even after everything we've won, this feeling never gets old,' he replied.

This was Roy's seventh time as a Premier League champion. Like Giggsy, he had been part of the early glory years, playing alongside Eric Cantona, Bryan Robson and Steve Bruce – and he had kept United on top as the team got younger, with David Beckham and the rest of the club's famous academy group bursting on to the scene. Roy had been the engine powering the Treble-winning season in 1999, and four years on he was still leading the squad, with deadly Dutch striker Ruud van Nistelrooy joining an experienced core.

He didn't usually allow himself to dwell on all these

achievements, but this latest title felt extra sweet.

The clock on the dressing room wall was ticking down towards kick-off, and when United manager Sir Alex Ferguson walked in, the noise quietened a little. Ferguson usually had that effect.

'I know you're all thinking about lifting the trophy again, and I am too,' Ferguson said. 'But let's finish it off in style, like proper champions do.'

Roy nodded. He hated to lose, and he knew he wouldn't enjoy the party later if United had a total no-show. Readjusting the captain's armband on his sleeve, he stood up and gulped down some water.

'Let's go, lads,' he said, heading for the tunnel.

The players walked out to a sea of blue around the stadium and a roar from the home fans, but this kind of atmosphere was nothing new for Roy or his teammates. Playing for Manchester United meant dealing with high pressure and high expectations – they were the team that everyone wanted to beat.

United would need that experience here after Everton scored from an early corner.

'Who was marking him?' Roy asked, looking around

at the other red shirts. 'Come on, wake up!'

Following Roy's example, United hit back. Soon they were flying forward and creating chances. A classic Beckham free kick made it 1–1 just before half-time.

'That's more like it!' Roy shouted while they celebrated near the corner flag.

Sitting down at half-time and wiping the sweat from his face, Roy considered how different the mood would be at that moment had United needed a win to clinch the title.

Everton were still looking dangerous in the second half, and Roy spent a lot of time running back into his own penalty area to help the defenders. Now they needed some magic at the other end of the pitch.

'One more big push!' he called to Giggsy and Ruud. 'They're getting tired.'

With just over ten minutes to go, Roy was still determined to find a winner. He played the ball forward to Giggsy, who flicked a pass through to Ruud. When Ruud turned his marker, he was dragged to the floor.

'Penalty!' Roy shouted, turning around just in time to see the referee pointing to the spot.

Ruud took the penalty himself and fired it into the net. Roy clenched his fist and jogged over to join the huddle of red shirts around Ruud. He could taste another victory.

When the final whistle sounded, Roy put his arms in the air. The past few months had felt like one long battle. He was exhausted.

Roy and his teammates headed into the tunnel for a few minutes while the trophy presentation was being prepared, and then they walked back onto the pitch, with the Everton players standing in two lines and clapping. He could hear the United fans in the corner of the stadium. They had all stayed behind to see their heroes lift the trophy.

The roar from the fans grew louder when Roy stepped forward to collect his medal. As he looked down at it, he felt the pride of being champions again. He knew the Premier League was getting more and more competitive, and he couldn't take anything for granted. He would be turning thirty-two that summer and his body was aching after every game these days.

Ferguson, who had now decided to delay his retirement plans, lifted the trophy and then brought it over to the players, handing it directly to Roy.

With his teammates jumping all around him, Roy raised the trophy into the air and screamed, 'Yeeeeaaaaah!'

Then the players continued their mini lap of honour, standing still just long enough for the photographers to snap some pictures.

'We've got our trophy back!' they sang. 'We've got our trophy back!'

In Roy's time at United, it had often felt that way. They had been the dominant team in English football, and that Premier League trophy had been a regular guest at Old Trafford. Every season felt a little different, but this had been a memorable one, with United saving some of their best performances for pressure-packed games in March and April. Those were the big games that would stick in his mind.

While Roy ran to catch up with his teammates, he reflected on his journey to the top and all his family and friends back in Ireland. The parties would be kicking off there too.

'What a ride!' he said to himself. 'And I'm not done yet!'

CHAPTER 2

A UNITED FAMILY

With the sound of thumping footsteps on the stairs, little Roy raced down for breakfast. Everyone was used to it by now – he was always on the move.

Johnson, one of his two older brothers, was already sitting in the kitchen.

'Roy, did you see the United score yesterday?' Johnson asked with a big grin.

Roy shook his head, but he could have probably guessed what it was from the look on his brother's face.

'United won again!' Johnson went on, triumphantly. 'Dad saw the goals on *Match of the Day* and said they were amazing.'

Roy rolled his eyes and sighed. There was no escaping Manchester United in the Keane family. His dad, Maurice, was a big fan, and so were his aunts and uncles and his brothers and lots of his cousins.

Whether it was scarves by the back door or a conversation on the phone or a poster in his brother's room, everything was United.

Roy couldn't even get away from it at school, where most of his best friends supported United or Liverpool or Celtic. Every boy pretended to be Bryan Robson or Kevin Keegan.

But Roy had his own ideas. When a friend's dad told him all about Tottenham and the fancy football they played, Roy decided that would be his team, even if that choice was met with some funny looks at home.

Later that week, Roy was sitting quietly at the back of the classroom, looking up at the clock on the wall as the seconds ticked by. The big hand was slowly creeping round towards the end of the school day, and the excitement was building. He could see two of his friends in the row in front were thinking the same thing – they would soon be on the pitch.

That had become their routine, putting their bags over their shoulders and rushing to the local football pitch in Mayfield. It didn't even matter about the weather. On the sunniest day or the rainiest day, they would be there. The bell sounded and they burst out of the door.

'Quick!' Roy said, pacing impatiently as one of his friends tied his shoelace. 'If we get there late, other kids will be playing.'

They raced out of the school, dodging past a few kids who seemed in no hurry to get home and gasping for breath as they turned the corner next to the pitch.

'We're the first ones here!' one of the boys shouted as they all saw the same thing: an empty field.

Roy had the ball in his bag, and they quickly picked teams, starting off with just six of them, then ten, then twelve. Before long, there were twenty boys charging around the pitch.

Those games were competitive, but nothing compared to the games in the street near Roy's house. From an early age, Roy had got used to competing there against older boys. He joined in with the street games whenever his older brothers and their friends let him play, and those matches went on and on until it got too dark to even see the ball.

Little Roy was usually right in the middle of the action, trying to keep up with kids twice his age. Of course, that sometimes ended with cuts and scrapes. His mum, Marie, would hurry to get a cloth to clean up his knees, reminding him that he didn't have to treat these games like the FA Cup final.

But Roy was fearless – and he could tell that he was becoming a better player.

'Nice tackle!' Johnson shouted during an evening game after Roy poked the ball away from one of the neighbours.

With a big grin, Roy sprinted forward. A boy on their team was dribbling past two defenders, but now he was trapped.

'In the middle!' Roy shouted, waving his arms to get the boy's attention. He guessed the boy wasn't really looking to play a pass but now he had no choice.

In a flash, the ball was coming towards Roy. He took a quick touch and kicked it as hard as he could. His eyes popped wide open in amazement when he saw the shot fly past the goalkeeper.

Goooooooooooooooooooooooaaaaaaaaaaaaaaaaaa aaaaaaalllllllllllllllllllllllllll!

Roy put his arms out and ran around in circles.

'Whoa, that was like a United goal!' Johnson called, running over and messing up Roy's hair.

'Seriously?' Roy replied. 'Does everything have to be about Manchester United?!'

At that stage, laughing at his brother's obsession, Roy had no idea that Manchester United would become an even bigger part of his life than he could ever have imagined.

CHAPTER 3

RISING WITH ROCKMOUNT

One afternoon, Roy was walking home with his mum when he spotted a boy across the road in a yellow-and-green football shirt.

'That's Rockmount!' Roy said suddenly, pointing. 'It's just like the ones that Denis and Johnson have.'

Marie looked over and saw that he was right. AFC Rockmount was one of the best clubs in their local city of Cork in the south of Ireland, though it was a bit unusual to see that shirt in their neighbourhood as most of the local boys played for Mayfield.

But Roy had taken a much bigger interest in Rockmount ever since his brothers had joined the youth teams there.

After the first practice, Roy was waiting at the door

when Denis and Johnson got home.

'What was it like?' he asked, forgetting to even say hello first.

'It's even better than the street games,' Denis explained. 'We did a warm-up, just like the professionals do, and then we did some dribbling drills and shooting practice.'

'Plus, we had a five-a-side game at the end,' Johnson added.

Roy wanted to hear every little detail.

A few years later, when it was time for Roy to decide on which club he would like to join, there's was only one choice: Rockmount.

From the moment he arrived for his first practice at Rockmount, Roy was in dreamland. The grass was nicely cut, the goalposts had nets that were well looked after and there were clean white lines around the edges of the pitch. This was real football, and he wasn't going to let this opportunity slip by.

Even with the Keane connection, there would be no easy ride with Rockmount. That was true in every sense, as Roy had to take the bus to get to practice.

Coach Murphy and Coach O'Sullivan had seen plenty of good young players step onto the grass at Rockmount's training pitch. That included some fantastic footballers who went on to play for the club for years, and many more kids who weren't quite good enough.

When Roy's name was mentioned, the coaches invited him to a training session with the Under 10s. Roy was only nine years old, and he looked even younger, but that session was the earliest chance for the coaches to see him in action.

Plenty of kids would have been scared to take on all the taller boys – some of them were a head taller than him. But Roy wasn't fazed.

'Who's brought their little brother to practice?' one of the boys shouted, looking at Roy and laughing.

Roy just stared back at him.

'Ignore him, Roy,' one of the other boys said. 'Kevin is always causing trouble.'

'Too late,' Roy thought to himself. Kevin had made the mistake of underestimating him.

The coaches split the boys into groups to work on

dribbling and passing. But when Coach Murphy set up a mini pitch for a game at the end, Roy saw his chance. Every time Kevin got the ball, Roy was there in a flash, taking it off his foot or sliding in.

Now that he had made it clear that he wouldn't be pushed around, Roy showed some of his other skills. He set up two goals with unselfish passes and then outsprinted two boys to score the last goal of the session.

He saw Coach Murphy and Coach O'Sullivan talking on the touchline – and he soon found out why. Rockmount wanted to sign him. Roy couldn't even hide his excitement.

'Yesssss!' he said, punching the air.

Coach Murphy saw Roy's quality and determination, and he decided to put Roy in the Under 11s to give him the best chance to develop quickly.

When Maurice and Marie heard the news, they couldn't help but wonder if their son was ready for that. Roy never let anyone push him around, but this was a big step for him.

'The coaches must think you're ready, but some of

the other boys are giants,' Marie said.

'Just watch, I'll outrun them all,' Roy replied, taking off his boots and trying not to get any mud on the carpet.

'It's the other teams that I feel bad for,' Maurice added, with a smile. 'They've got to go up against Roy.'

But there were no easy days in practice with so many good players at Rockmount. While Roy was dribbling around before the start of one training session, he looked up and saw two of his teammates, Alan and Paul, juggling the ball with little flicks. They used their feet, thighs, chests and heads to keep it in the air. Roy wished he could do that so effortlessly.

In the mini games, the speed of the passing was a surprise at first. When he played against his school friends, Roy could chase the ball and close people down, but he had to adjust at Rockmount or else he would be running around in circles.

Rockmount games quickly became the highlight of Roy's week, and he proved his coaches right with brilliant performances in midfield. The Under 11s piled up wins on the way to a league and cup double.

There was plenty to celebrate – and Roy had heard all about Rockmount's end-of-season party. All the different age groups were invited for food, awards and music.

The Under 11s found a table in the corner, telling jokes and shrieking with laughter. Then they saw Coach Murphy walking onto the stage.

'Woooooooo!' they all cheered, when Coach Murphy waved in their direction.

They had already collected their medals for winning the cup, but they were excited to get their trophies for winning the league. One by one, their names were called out and they walked up, shook hands with Coach Murphy and carried their trophies back to their seats.

After Coach Murphy had called up each player, he picked up the microphone again. 'Congratulations to all the boys on a great year,' he said. 'I've got one last award to give out tonight, and that's our Under 11 Player of the Year trophy.'

The room went a little quieter.

'This year, the award goes to . . . Roy Keane.'

Roy almost dropped his drink in shock. He looked around at his teammates and then across at his parents, who were sitting at the table opposite and clapping proudly.

'Come on up, Roy,' Coach Murphy said.

Roy weaved between tables to get back to the stage. Everyone turned to look at him, and he felt his cheeks going a little red.

When he saw the trophy in Coach Murphy's hands, Roy's eyes lit up. There was a golden figure swinging to take a shot, standing on top of a giant ball.

'Well done, Roy,' Coach Murphy said. 'You had an unbelievable season. Rockmount is lucky to have you.'

'Thanks, Coach,' Roy replied. 'I'm really happy to be here, and I'm already counting the days until next season.'

CHAPTER 4

MIDFIELD MENACE

The Rockmount coaches quickly saw that there was much more to Roy's game than just running and tackling. He had good control and his passing improved with every training session.

Rockmount had other players to dribble and score goals, and Roy was fine with that. He understood that controlling the midfield and winning the ball back were what he did best, and he was just happy to do his part to help Rockmount win.

'We're an unbeatable team when you're playing like that,' Coach O'Sullivan told Roy, as they walked off the pitch together after another win.

'I should have taken a shot at the end there instead of trying the through ball,' Roy replied.

Coach O'Sullivan smiled. That was classic Roy. He never got caught up in praise from the coaches or the other players. Instead, he was usually kicking himself about a small detail, something that he could have done better.

Roy still liked to get forward when he could, making runs from midfield. That often seemed to catch defenders by surprise, and he was usually fast enough to beat them to the ball in a sprint.

But he knew he had to score more goals once he got into the box. He needed more shooting practice, and that meant persuading his younger brother Pat to come over to the pitch in Mayfield with him.

'I guess I'm the goalie again?' Pat asked, pretending to be annoyed.

'You're getting really good,' Roy said, trying to encourage him.

'Well, I should be, with all the practice you're giving me!' Pat replied, laughing.

For the next hour, Roy took shot after shot from just inside the penalty area.

At first, he was going for power. But the ball ended

up all over the place. Some shots flew into the net, but even more went over the bar or wide of the post.

Roy shook his head. He needed better accuracy. As he lined up another shot, he practised the kind of technique he wanted.

'Okay, let's try this again,' he said, as Pat got ready on the goal line.

Roy placed the ball and took a couple of steps back. This time, he went for a little less power and guided the ball with the inside of his foot. His shot skidded along the grass and bounced in off the post.

He repeated it on the next few shots, sweeping the ball into the bottom corners, away from Pat's dives. That was much better.

All the work paid off. Roy scored two goals in the next game, pointing over to Pat on the touchline and giving him a thumbs up.

After the latest cup victory, Roy added another medal to the shelf in his room. It had become quite a collection, with Rockmount brushing aside all the other local teams. Suddenly, his weekends had been completely taken over by football.

'You'll just about have time to eat, have a shower and sleep,' Marie teased. 'You're playing for the Under 11s, Under 12s and Under 13s this weekend.'

'Luckily, there's no such thing as too much football,' Roy shot back with a smile.

But on Sunday nights, he was usually too tired to do anything, apart from lie down on the sofa.

A few weeks later, the Under 13s coaches were looking at the fixture list, and they saw that their next game was against one of their biggest rivals.

'That's going to be a tough game,' one of the coaches said. 'We'll need Roy for that one.'

'Are you sure?' another coach answered. 'He's been playing well but this is Under 13s and he's only eleven.'

'That boy can handle the heat,' Coach Murphy added, appearing in the doorway. 'He's good enough, and I'm never worried about Roy when the game gets physical. He loves that.'

Sure enough, Roy was the man of the match. He was first to every loose ball, he won every 50-50 tackle and he even started the move for Rockmount's second goal with a quick pass out to the wing.

'Roy's ball!' he yelled, appearing out of nowhere to intercept another pass in the final minutes. Rockmount were hanging on to the lead, and he found an extra burst of energy. He was still charging around when other boys were complaining about cramp in their legs or breathing heavily.

'You're not tired, are you?' Roy asked with a cheeky grin as he ran past one of the boys, who was bent over with his hands on his knees.

Rockmount powered to win yet another league and cup double, and Roy was in the middle of it all. It didn't seem to matter what age group he was playing in. He was always ready.

Roy still wasn't the most skilful player in the team, or the biggest or the fastest, but no one could control the game like him. It wasn't just people around Cork who were paying attention now. The Ireland youth team scouts were starting to take notice too.

CHAPTER 5

DUBLIN DESPAIR

Roy never had to look far for his next game of football, from the playground to the Mayfield pitch to the local streets. But for once, it was all quiet on his walk home from school.

He took off his jumper and put it in his backpack, as he turned into his street.

'You made it, son!' a voice shouted in the distance.

Roy looked up and squinted. It was his dad, standing on the pavement, leaning against a lamppost and waving his arm. For a second, Roy wondered if something was wrong. He walked a bit faster.

But as Roy got closer, he could see that there was no worry on his dad's face. Instead, there was a huge smile. In his right hand, he was holding a newspaper.

'You made it!' he said again, handing over the newspaper.

Roy glanced at it and immediately understood. There was a short section listing all the boys selected for the Ireland Under 15 trials in Dublin, and there he was – R. Keane.

Wow! Roy jumped in the air. He felt he was having a good season at Rockmount, and it was great to see that other people agreed with him.

But Roy also knew from experience that there were no guarantees with trials. It had been a disappointing experience the previous year when he went to the Under 14 trials and wasn't selected. He was stronger and faster now – maybe that would make the difference.

While Roy was waiting on the train station platform with Rockmount teammates Alan and Len, he felt some nerves about the trials, but those were soon swept aside by the excitement of this adventure.

'The train to Dublin should be here in about five minutes!' a man in a uniform called out.

They spent the journey swapping stories and telling

jokes, but they all got a little quieter when the train chugged into Dublin station.

They found their way to the field for the trials and saw lots of other boys. One of the coaches had a clipboard with a list of players, and he put a little tick next to each of their names.

By now, Roy knew how it worked at the trials. There were boys from schools all over the country and, once they had all been registered, they were split into four teams, each with a different colour bib.

Roy was on the green team, and he hoped that was a good sign. He wasn't with Alan or Len, who were both walking over to the pitch opposite.

Roy was one of the two central midfielders for his team, playing next to a tall boy with really short hair.

'I'm Connor,' he said, shaking hands with Roy. 'Ready to dominate?'

Roy smiled. He was always ready for football.

One of the coaches placed the ball in the centre circle and then retreated to the touchline to take notes.

'Play!' he called out.

The next hour was similar to what Roy remembered

from his Under 14s trials. There were some good moments where one of the teams produced a few nice passes, but there was no real connection. Most of the boys had never played together before and there were a lot of long punts down the pitch.

It wasn't like Roy's Rockmount games. In those matches, he knew where his teammates would be, and they understood when Roy would be making his bursting runs from midfield.

But he focused on doing all the basics right. He won headers and crunched into tackles, leaving one boy on the ground. When the green team lost the ball, Roy led the chase to get it back.

'Nice work, Roy,' one of the coaches said, shaking his hand as he was subbed off for another boy.

Watching the final few minutes, Roy reflected on his performance. Overall, he was pleased. It had been solid rather than spectacular, but he had done a lot of the same things that the coaches loved at Rockmount. Sweat was still pouring down his face and he knew he couldn't have worked any harder.

He swapped notes with Alan and Len on the train

home. It sounded like there had been more goals in their game, but Roy wasn't sure what that meant for his chances of earning one of the midfield spots.

'So, how did it go?' Marie asked as Roy arrived home and took off his jacket.

'Pretty good,' Roy replied. 'I did my best. If that wasn't what the coaches were looking for, good luck to them.'

Marie smiled. That was typical Roy.

All he could do was wait. Eventually, Alan and Len received letters to confirm their places in the squad, but nothing arrived in the post for Roy. He knew what that meant.

There was no chance for Roy to ask the Ireland Under 15s scouts or coaches about why he wasn't selected, but he guessed that they thought he was too small to play in midfield.

Roy was confused. Didn't they value a strong tackler and a non-stop runner? He knew he was a better player than Connor and the other midfielders in his trial match. He wondered if they had made it into the squad.

'We're gutted for you, Roy,' Coach Murphy said, putting an arm round him before the next Rockmount practice. 'I'm a bit biased, but I'd always want someone like you in my team. Still, there's always next year's trials, so keep your head up.'

Roy congratulated Alan and Len, but this setback really stung. Making the team would have confirmed that Roy was on the right track as a footballer, but now he was left with doubts. And as he prepared for his next game with Rockmount, the frustration was building.

CHAPTER 6

TIME FOR PLAN B

There was always plenty of excitement whenever a local player was signed by an English club, and so Roy heard all the details when other boys landed their dream moves.

As he thought about his own future, that kind of breakthrough felt a long way away. Sure, his youth team performances for Rockmount had brought more trophies and more pats on the back from his coaches, but he was still playing in Cork – not in London or Manchester or Liverpool.

The months dragged on, and Roy grew restless. He still wanted to be a professional footballer, and he knew he was struggling at school, but what was he going to do next? As he moved on from the Under 17s, he could see his options shrinking.

'I'm just drifting,' Roy admitted one night when he sat down with his parents. 'I need a plan.'

'Well, don't make any big decisions yet,' Marie replied. 'You could apply for some trials with English clubs and then work for a few months while you wait for replies.'

Roy nodded, but he knew it wasn't easy to find work anywhere in Cork at that moment.

'No matter what, keep believing,' Marie added. 'If football is your future, another opportunity will come.'

A few months later, Roy was finding it harder and harder to see how things were going to turn around for him. To drag himself out of the house and earn a little money, he took whatever jobs he could get, including some weeks picking potatoes.

As he lifted another bag of potatoes and carried it back to his bike, he sighed. He was grateful for the job and his boss had been really kind, but none of this was what he had pictured when he was rising through the Rockmount youth teams.

Some of his old teammates tried to cheer him up.

Alan was playing in England now, but they still kept in touch.

'Don't give up,' Alan reminded him. 'Keep training, keep playing and someone is going to jump at the chance to sign you. You just need a little luck to go your way.'

Roy agreed and tried to sound more positive, but inside he was starting to doubt whether a career in football was really in his future. Maybe he had missed his chance.

But then a whole new option landed in front of him at the perfect moment. The Football Association in Ireland were launching a new program. If Roy joined it, he would be training in Dublin during the week and earning some money at the same time. He wouldn't quite become a professional footballer, but he would be inching closer.

Spots were limited, though, and once again Roy found himself as the odd man out. When he realised that he would need a new club to register him for the program, his body went numb. Another door had been slammed in his face.

Or had it?

His original plan had been to register for the program as a Cork City player. But when that fell through, Eddie O'Rourke at Cobh Ramblers heard about Roy's situation and wanted to help.

'Hang on a minute,' Eddie said. He remembered Roy from his Rockmount days. 'If the Cork City paperwork hasn't gone through, you could sign for Cobh and join the program.'

Roy sat up in his chair. 'Really?'

Eddie had to double check with the other Cobh coaches, so Roy waited nervously next to the phone for hours. Finally, he got the call – and it was good news. He would get a spot on the Football Association program if he signed with Cobh, while also playing for the Ramblers' youth teams at the weekends. Putting his signature on the contract was the easiest decision Roy had made in a long time.

'This could be exactly what I've been waiting for,' Roy explained excitedly, talking his parents through everything he knew about the program.

'I told you!' Marie said, grinning. 'You just had to

keep believing!'

When a package arrived in the post with all the details about the program, Roy couldn't wait to get started. Soon he was on the train station platform again, waiting for the train to Dublin.

That brought back some difficult memories for Roy, and some of the nerves started to kick in. He knew this might be his last chance to break through as a footballer. He was seventeen and still looking for the move that would take his career to the next level. If this didn't work out, he might be back picking potatoes.

As he heard the train approaching, he promised himself that he would give every ounce of energy to turn his dreams into reality.

CHAPTER 7

THE BIG BREAKTHROUGH

'Where's the bus?' Roy asked, shaking his head and pacing around. 'We're going to be late.'

Roy and his Cobh Ramblers teammates were waiting in the car park for the trip to face Belvedere Boys in the Under 18s Cup. Except, well, there was a real chance now that they might miss kick-off.

'I'm calling the bus company again,' one of the coaches said. 'The driver was supposed to be here thirty minutes ago.'

Roy watched the traffic, but it was just cars and trucks rushing past. He had woken up in a great mood, brushing off a busy week on the FAS program and focusing on this big game, but now the travel plans seemed to be falling apart.

The bus finally arrived, with the driver frantically explaining that he had got lost somewhere along the way. Roy and his teammates rushed up the steps as fast as they could.

It would take a few hours to get to Dublin, and Roy was watching the clock all the way. At one stage, the roads looked clear, and he relaxed a little. But then they were stuck in slow traffic, and the restlessness returned. Roy couldn't tell if the coaches were joking when they suggested that the players could start some stretches in their seats.

This wasn't how any of them had pictured the warm-up, but they had no choice. When they arrived at the pitch at last, there was barely enough time to change and drink some water.

It might not have mattered so much against a weaker opponent, but Belvedere were a really good team. The first leg had been a tight battle, with Roy scoring Cobh's goal in a 1–1 draw, and the second leg would be even tougher, especially without a proper warm-up.

While Belvedere looked fresh, Cobh started the game like a team that had just got off a bus. They were

3–0 down in a flash.

With the match slipping away, Roy refused to give up. He wasn't even thinking about the score anymore. He just wanted to make a point and show that Cobh belonged on the same pitch as Belvedere.

For the rest of the game, Roy was a blur of action, intercepting passes, thundering into tackles, and winning headers against taller players. Most of all, he kept running and running and running, powered by the frustration of the day.

Even losing 4–0 in the final minutes, Roy was sprinting to close down Belvedere players. He left the pitch with his head down and his shoulders slumped, but he had battled until the end.

Roy took off his socks and shin pads and sat quietly in the corner of the small dressing room. No one had much to say after that scoreline, and the coaches could tell this wasn't the moment for a detailed review of the loss.

'Hit the showers and we'll get some food across the road before we drive back,' one of the coaches said eventually, sensing the players were all frozen in shock.

Roy's legs were aching as he walked into the café, and he winced as he sat down. He was really hungry, and a plate of hot food instantly put a thankful grin on his face.

As he took the last bite and reached for his glass of water, Roy looked up and saw the Cobh Ramblers vice-chairman approaching his table. The vice-chairman walked over to Roy, leaning down and lowering his voice.

'One good thing might have come out of tonight after all,' he said. 'There was a Nottingham Forest scout called Noel at the game tonight, and he'd like to invite you for a trial.'

Roy's eyes popped wide open. He started to smile, but then stopped himself. This sort of thing just didn't seem to work out for him. He had got his hopes up too many times before.

But he didn't want to be negative about it either. He was just being realistic and a little cautious.

'I'm definitely interested,' he finally said. 'Can you give them my phone number? Let's see if they actually call.'

This time, there was no waiting by the phone. Roy

just got on with training and spending time with his friends whenever he was back in Cork. He was playing for the Cobh senior team at the weekends and testing himself against grown men.

'Here we go again,' he thought, realising that a whole week had passed with no news from Forest.

It was almost a surprise in the end when he got the call from Noel, the Forest scout. Roy was relieved that Noel couldn't see the big smile on his face as he listened to all the arrangements for the trial.

That night, when his parents got home, Roy joined them in the hallway.

'How was your day, Roy?' his dad asked.

'Pretty good,' Roy replied, not giving anything away. 'I was just on my way upstairs to pack.'

His parents glanced at each other, then at Roy.

'Where are you going?' his mum asked, looking confused.

'Oh, didn't I mention it?' Roy said with a big smile. 'I've got a trial with Nottingham Forest.'

'What?!' his parents both said at once.

'There was a scout at the Belvedere game and he

called today,' Roy explained.

'That's amazing, Roy,' his dad said, putting an arm round him. 'You really deserve this.'

Roy nodded. 'Yeah, I feel like I've waited long enough for it,' he said. 'But it's a trial, not a contract. I've got to show them why they should take a chance on me.'

After a couple of mix-ups with Forest, Roy got his train ticket to join the reserve team squad at the start of the next season. Once he was finally in Nottingham, he felt good. This was the right place for him at the right time.

Roy was introduced to the other reserve team players, and he was happy to see the coaches explaining some running drills to start the session. He knew he could match anyone in those.

Then there were a few rounds of the midfielders and forwards trying to score against the defenders, followed by some 3 v 3 mini games. But he knew his best chance to make an impression would be in a real eleven-a-side game to show what he could do on a big pitch. Roy grinned when one of the coaches told him about a trial game at the weekend – this was his moment.

He jumped up and down as he waited for kick-off, and he immediately saw he was hungrier than the other midfielders. This was his whole football future on the line, and he was on a mission.

After Roy slid into a crunching tackle, he noticed the other midfielders backed away the next time the ball bounced loose. He had control of the midfield, covering back to help the defence, then appearing out of nowhere on the edge of the box at the other end seconds later.

Roy still didn't know his teammates very well, but that didn't matter. He had played enough football by now to adjust to the situation. He ran until his legs burned and when he was subbed off, he sat down on the bench and tried not to show how tired he was.

But a little smile was creeping onto his face. He was usually very honest with himself when it came to reviewing his performances. If he had a bad game, he could admit it. If he was just okay, he wasn't afraid to say that either. But today he knew he had been brilliant.

Sure enough, the Forest coaches called him over at

the end of the next training session.

'We'd like to offer you a contract, Roy,' the head youth coach said. 'You've really impressed us, and we think you'll have a bright future at Forest.'

The rest of the discussions were out of Roy's hands. Forest and Cobh would have to agree on a transfer fee. Roy kept his fingers crossed. He had told his parents and hoped they would keep it quiet, but he had a feeling that half of Cork might know about it by now.

Roy was still in Nottingham when Brian Clough, the legendary manager who had led Forest to two European Cups, met with the Cobh management team to negotiate the transfer fee.

After all of the ups and downs, Roy felt ready to seize this chance. He had taken the long route to England's top division, but he had made it – and nothing was going to stop him now.

CHAPTER 8

A DAY OF SURPRISES

When Roy arrived at training on a rainy Tuesday morning, he looked at the clock in his car. He was early, as usual.

He was enjoying life at Forest. It was still such a thrill to be doing what he loved every day, and he could see the improvements in his game – his control in tight spaces, his vision, his movement. He was training with the reserves but also learning from being around veteran first-team players like Stuart Pearce and Des Walker.

'No one is going to work harder than me,' Roy had told the Forest coaches when he joined the club. So far, he was keeping that promise. While some of the reserve team players were older or unhappy about not getting more first team opportunities, Roy had a smile on his face every day.

Roy waved to one of the reserve team coaches on his way to get changed, then went through a few stretches. One by one, his teammates joined him on the pitch and he passed the ball around with two of the other youngsters, Scot Gemmill and Phil Starbuck.

But that was the end of the normal part of his day. From then onwards, everything felt like it was out of a comic.

'Roy and Phil, I need a word with you two,' said Ronnie Fenton, one of the senior coaches, signalling for them to follow him.

Roy looked at Phil. 'Do you think we're in trouble?' he asked, as they started to walk off.

Phil hesitated, then grinned. 'I doubt it, unless it's about your terrible tackle on me last week,' he said, with a wink.

'I got the ball and you know it!' Roy fired back, laughing too.

Ronnie perched on the edge of a table and pointed for Roy and Phil to sit down. He got straight to the point. 'You boys are going with the first team to Liverpool for tonight's game at Anfield,' he explained.

Roy froze. It was like his whole body had switched off for a second. Had he misheard? Anfield? Tonight?

But he wasn't imagining it. Ronnie went through the details quickly. The rest of the squad was already on the way to Liverpool, so he would be driving Roy and Phil to the game.

Roy rushed home to pack a bag. His head was still spinning. One minute he was smiling about the news; the next minute the nerves kicked in. He was about to be thrown into the dressing room with all the famous first team players.

'We've just got to pick up the manager on the way,' Ronnie said as they set off.

Roy looked at Phil. 'We're picking up Brian Clough?' he asked. The day just kept getting stranger.

Sure enough, the car turned into a side street and stopped outside a house.

Ronnie turned to Roy.

'Roy, ring the bell and let him know we're here,' he said.

Roy slowly got out of the car, wondering if this was

all some kind of prank. He pressed the bell. When the door opened, there was Brian Clough.

'Come in,' he said. 'I need five more minutes.'

So, Roy stood there in his manager's kitchen, waiting in silence.

'This is the Irishman I was telling you about,' Clough said to his wife as he hurried through the house.

Roy smiled politely and shook hands. No one was going to believe this story.

When they finally got to Anfield, Roy and Phil walked through the players' entrance and into the dressing room. Roy dropped off his bag and tried to take in everything that was happening. He felt like he was in some kind of dream.

'Get ready, lads,' Ronnie called out. 'The warm-up starts in fifteen minutes.'

That snapped Roy out of it, and he rushed to get changed. Walking down the tunnel to warm up, he felt the same rush of excitement that he used to feel on his birthday when he was a kid.

'It's so cool that Forest do this for young players,' he said to Phil. 'What an experience to travel with the squad and get a glimpse of life in the first team.'

Roy had been realistic from the moment he got the news that morning. Forest were putting him on the bench, but surely he wasn't *actually* going to play in a big game like this. He didn't even really know the first team players and he was still introducing himself to some of them as they all jogged across the pitch, following Ronnie's instructions.

After the warm-up, some of the players huddled around talking in the dressing room. Others preferred to drink water and clear their heads in silence.

Roy wasn't sure what to do, but he didn't want to just sit there looking shy or getting in the way. When he spotted the kit man laying out the shirts and shorts, he jumped up and started to help him.

'Roy, what are you doing?' a voice boomed out from across the room.

He turned to see Brian Clough staring at him.

'I was . . . well, I thought I'd . . .' Roy mumbled.

'Take that Number 7 shirt and see how it looks on you,' Clough called.

Roy paused. Was this some kind of joke? No one

seemed to be laughing, so he picked up the shirt and put it on.

Clough walked over and stopped in front of Roy. 'Looks good!' he said. 'You better start on the right wing then.'

Roy laughed and started to take off the shirt, ready for whoever was really playing on the right wing.

'I'm serious, Roy,' Clough said, putting a hand on his shoulder. 'You've been terrific with the reserves. Just play the same way here. Get up and down the pitch, and make sure you enjoy this moment.'

Roy was speechless for the second time that day. But there was no time to think about how or why this was happening. He had to focus. In less than thirty minutes, he would be making his Forest debut at Anfield against Liverpool. Maybe this was better than having days to think about it.

He took a deep breath and stood up straight in the tunnel. The Liverpool players appeared, and Roy was suddenly standing next to some of the best players in the country. He spotted John Barnes and Ian Rush and Peter Beardsley.

But tonight, they were the opponents. Sure, they were great players, but he wasn't going to waste any time thinking about their reputations. His only job was to stop them.

Roy knew he wasn't a typical right winger, with dribbling runs and lightning pace. He didn't usually play on the wing. But he understood his job that night – running, tackling and keeping an eye on Barnes.

That's what he did. In the first few minutes, Liverpool won the ball in midfield and quickly played it out to Barnes. Roy was there in a flash with a hard tackle that sent Barnes flying.

'Good work, Roy,' Clough called from the touchline.

He didn't have many chances to push forward, but he had worked non-stop to close down the Liverpool players.

Though Forest lost 2–0, nothing could shake Roy out of his happy mood. It was the kind of performance that confirmed he would be playing at this level for many years to come, and as he left Anfield behind, he felt like he was walking on air.

CHAPTER 9

FOREST HIGHS AND LOWS

Before long, Roy had become a regular in a Forest team that was chasing trophies. He was still learning about life as a professional footballer, but Brian Clough was giving him the chance to figure out those answers on the pitch.

'Control the ball, pass the ball and keep running.' That was Clough's guidance.

Roy grinned when he thought about a great manager like Clough telling him that, yet all those coaches at his youth team trials had never appreciated his ability to do exactly that.

Forest's strikers weren't the fastest in the league, so

their best moves came from Roy's midfield runs. When Nigel Jemson or Teddy Sheringham held off defenders and turned into space, that was the signal for Roy to burst behind the defence, ready for a through ball.

He had to be patient, though. Sometimes the pass was intercepted. Sometimes it didn't come at all. But he kept making the runs because he could see the panic it caused for defences.

Roy was a game-changer in that season's FA Cup semi-final when Forest took on West Ham. He set up the first goal, appearing on the edge of the box for a quick layoff, and he was on the move again when Gary Crosby pushed forward down the right wing.

When Crosby sent a cross into the box, Roy was in a full sprint. He watched the ball carefully and slid forward to poke a shot into the net.

Goooooooooooooooooooooooaaaaaaaaaaaaaaaaaaaa aaaaaaalllllllllllllllllllllllllllll!

Roy put his arms in the air in front of the Forest fans while his teammates crowded around him.

He was getting used to playing in big games, with his football career moving faster than he had ever expected.

He had to pinch himself to believe this was all real. Forest won the semi-final 4–0 and Roy grinned at the thought of what that meant: they were going to Wembley!

He couldn't wait to play at the famous stadium. Just two years before, he had been picking potatoes and stacking boxes, and now he was going to be playing in the FA Cup final against Tottenham.

But that dream was thrown into doubt when he limped off in a league game just before the final. His ankle felt even worse the next morning. Suddenly, he was in a race against time to be fit for the biggest game of his life.

Roy tried ice and rest to give himself the best chance, and he was determined to play, even if that meant taping up his ankle and living with the pain for ninety minutes.

'I'm ready,' he told the Forest coaches.

He didn't sleep well the night before the final, but he still felt the nervous excitement flowing through his body when he joined his teammates on the bus. He tried to take it all in – the journey through the streets around the stadium, with lots of Forest fans cheering and waving, and his first sight of the Wembley pitch. He knew the whole country would be watching today.

'Remember to have some fun out there,' Des Walker told him, sensing that Roy might be feeling a little shaky. 'Football is supposed to be fun.'

Roy felt calmer as he stood in the tunnel, but the atmosphere in the packed stadium still blew him away when they walked out. Wow! Somehow, he hadn't quite expected it.

But the big day had a heartbreaking ending. Things looked good when Stuart fired Forest into the lead with an unstoppable free kick – and even when Mark Crossley saved Gary Lineker's penalty.

Then the game flipped. Tottenham hit back in the second half, and they were on top as the match headed into extra-time. Even with his ankle slowing him down, Roy chased every ball. Forest had made their two allowed substitutions by now, so he knew he had to keep going.

A Tottenham corner looped towards the back post and Roy turned just in time to see Des diving to try to clear it. But Des was facing the net, and his header floated up into the top corner. An own goal!

Des was devastated. They all were. Tottenham hung on for the 2–1 win, and Roy just sat on the pitch, trying to shake the horrible feeling of losing a cup final. He had always been on the winning side in his Rockmount finals. It left all the Forest players a little numb heading into the summer break.

By now, Roy had played a few games for the Ireland youth teams, putting the disappointment of the schoolboy trials behind him. All the youth coaches seemed to believe in him now, and he had represented the Under 19s and the Under 21s.

The only remaining step was for Roy to join the Ireland senior team, and he got the call-up for a friendly against Chile that summer. It was a proud moment, and he knew how much it meant to his family and friends back in Ireland.

It also reminded him again how much he missed them all. Clough had been really supportive about letting Roy go back to Cork for a few days when he felt really homesick, trusting him to be ready to play at the weekends.

But Roy liked Nottingham too, especially after he met a girl called Theresa who would soon become a big part of his life. Although he didn't make the best first impression, luckily Theresa didn't give up on him.

The next season, Forest bounced back with another good cup run – this time in the League Cup. The rain was pouring down at White Hart Lane as Forest got a chance for payback against Tottenham in the semi-final. But a delayed kick-off left the players sitting restlessly in the dressing room.

When they were finally able to get on to the pitch, Roy passed the ball around with Scot and Des. The ball instantly got stuck in the mud.

'It's going to be a scrappy game,' Roy said, pointing to the mud. But he had a little smile on his face too, because he loved these kinds of games. 'Now we'll see who really wants to win.'

Roy was still only twenty but he was fearless. Once the game started, he was soon covered in mud. That didn't stop him sliding into another tackle and bursting forward. He was going to need his endless supply of energy, though, as the game finished 1–1 and the teams prepared for thirty minutes of extra-time.

'Stick together out there and we'll be fine,' Clough told his players. 'Remember last year's final. Let's show we want it more than them.'

Forest won a corner on the right and Roy jogged into the box. He wasn't even close to being their tallest player, but he won his share of headers. He had made the same run for a couple of corners earlier in the game, but the ball hadn't reached him. As the ball floated across towards the penalty spot, he sensed it could be third time lucky.

With a quick dart forward, he left his defender standing like a statue and jumped to thump a header into the top corner.

Goooooooooooooooooooooooaaaaaaaaaaaaaaaaaaaaaaaaaalllllllllllllllllllllllllllll!

'Come on!' he shouted, racing towards the section of Forest fans and sliding on his knees.

'What a header!' Des called, wrapping him in a muddy hug.

This time, it was Forest's turn to celebrate an extra-time win. Roy found the match ball at the end and kept it for his collection.

But that semi-final joy was followed by another runners-up medal when Forest lost the final to Manchester United. Even though they had played some great games that year, Roy felt the familiar burn of disappointment on the journey back to Nottingham.

It felt like Forest were heading in the right direction after those finals in 1991 and 1992, but this 1992–93 season was one long nightmare. With standards slipping, the team slid down the Premier League table and into a nail-biting relegation battle.

'They're too good to get relegated,' everyone said. But Roy knew the truth. Forest were sinking, and they had run out of time to save themselves.

Roy had signed a new contract with Forest earlier in the season, but after Clough announced that he would be leaving the club, it felt like the end of an era for everyone – and that included Roy.

CHAPTER 10

TRANSFER TWISTS

That summer, Roy knew there were some big decisions ahead. First, though, he had to process the shock and embarrassment of Forest's relegation. Could they have worked harder?

'We've let the fans down,' Roy told his parents on a visit back to Cork.

'You gave it your all, Roy,' Marie said, giving him a hug. 'You always do. You don't know any other way to play. But there's nothing you can do now. Just focus on next season.'

Roy nodded. She was right. But thinking about next season brought more questions and unknowns.

He had a relegation clause in his contract which meant he would be allowed to leave if another team agreed to pay the transfer fee – and there were lots of rumours about Premier League clubs wanting to sign him.

Blackburn were interested, and he knew they had contacted Forest in the past. When they made an offer, Roy met with manager Kenny Dalglish to learn more. He liked what he heard.

'We're building something special,' Kenny said. 'With you in midfield, I really believe we can reach the next level and compete for the title.'

This was exciting, Roy thought. Blackburn were getting better and better every year, and he really wanted to stay in the Premier League.

The conversation drifted from topic to topic, and so, by the time the deal was done, it was too late at night to get the paperwork filled in. They would have to wait until Monday. Still, Roy was in a great mood as he travelled back to Ireland to meet up with his friends.

The next morning, Roy stirred when the phone rang downstairs. He had no idea what time it was, but he knew he had gone to bed really late.

He waited, hoping someone else would answer the

phone. It was starting to give him a headache. At last, he heard footsteps and then Pat's voice. 'Hello?'

Then there was a long pause, as if Pat was struggling to understand what the caller was saying.

'Erm, yes of course, just hold on a minute,' Pat said eventually, stumbling over the words then dropping the phone and running upstairs.

'Roy! Roy!' he shouted, running into the room.

Roy sat up in bed, his heart racing. 'What's happened?' he asked.

Pat caught his breath, then a big grin spread across his face. 'The phone call is for you,' he said.

Roy looked back at him in total confusion. 'Well, who is it?'

'Someone you might have heard of . . . his name is Alex Ferguson.'

Roy felt his jaw drop. He rolled out of bed and rushed to the phone. Thankfully, Ferguson hadn't hung up yet.

'Roy, I'll get right to the point, we want you at United,' Ferguson explained. 'We've been watching you closely at Forest and you'd fit really well in our midfield.'

A hundred thoughts raced through Roy's head.

'Well, I've agreed to sign for Blackburn,' he mumbled.

'Have you signed anything yet?' Ferguson asked.

'Well, no,' Roy replied. 'They're getting the contract ready for Monday.'

'Okay, good, come up to Manchester this weekend,' Ferguson added, before Roy could say anything else. 'Let's talk, and then you can make your decision.'

This changed everything. With his family sounding even more excited than he was, Roy packed a bag for the trip to Manchester.

'This is amazing!' Johnson said, bursting into the room. 'As your older brother, I should probably come and visit you every weekend!'

When Roy arrived at Ferguson's house, they spent the next few hours talking about the club, the vision for the future and why Roy had to be part of it. United had just won the Premier League, but Bryan Robson was coming towards the end of his career, and they would need a replacement.

Roy couldn't help but smile while Ferguson outlined all the advantages of signing with United. He could really see himself doing well there.

'I told Blackburn that I'd sign for them,' Roy told his parents when he got home. 'But how can I turn down the chance to join Manchester United?!'

'You've got to make the best decision for you, Roy,' they advised. 'There might be some hurt feelings – but think about what's going to make you happiest.'

Roy went upstairs and lay down on the bed, staring at the ceiling as if it might provide the answer. After twenty minutes, he had decided what he wanted to do, but it all felt so messy.

Finally, he made the phone call he was dreading, letting Kenny and Blackburn know that he had changed his mind and wanted to sign with United instead. As he expected, they weren't pleased.

There were still more twists and turns, but Forest and United finally agreed on a £3.75m transfer fee. Overnight, Roy had become Britain's most expensive footballer, and he was about to enter a whole new world with the Premier League champions.

CHAPTER 11

A DREAM START AT UNITED

There was a sign on the door in front of him: a Manchester United logo and the words *Meeting Room*. Roy gulped, then took a deep breath and pushed the door open.

He was slightly relieved when he saw that the room wasn't yet crammed with familiar, famous faces. Even so, Bryan 'Robbo' Robson, Steve Bruce and Mark Hughes were already there. All three of them looked round to see who had walked in, and Roy could feel his stomach doing backflips.

Roy could even be shy around his friends sometimes, so the idea of starting up a conversation with such legendary United players was already making him sweaty.

Thankfully, Steve broke the silence. 'Welcome to United, Roy!' he said, crossing the room to shake hands. 'We're excited to have you here and it's great that you were able to join us on the tour.'

It had been non-stop for Roy ever since signing with United, with a flight to South Africa to join up with the United squad for some preseason friendlies. It was a chance to get to know his new teammates on the pitch and at the evening events that had been arranged.

Roy had prepared himself for the big step up at United, but he still found himself starstruck when he saw the quality of the other players. At one end of the training pitch, Eric Cantona was scoring volley after volley with just a casual swing of his right leg. On the far side, Ryan Giggs was dribbling faster than anyone Roy had ever seen. Everyone called him 'Giggsy' and he was even younger than Roy, but he had become one of the most exciting wingers in the league.

Despite feeling like he had a lot to work on, every training session was football paradise for Roy. Assistant manager Brian Kidd came up with creative drills and Roy was soon passing the ball almost as effortlessly as Eric and Giggsy in the warm-up.

But there were still some days when he trudged off the pitch reflecting on his mistakes or limited contributions in the mini games, and wondering whether he would ever get into the first team.

'Don't be too hard on yourself,' his dad told him. 'United signed you for a reason, and you'll improve even faster around great players.'

As the weeks passed, Roy's teammates did their best to make him feel like part of the team. He hadn't expected them to go to so much effort. Steve and Robbo invited him for a meal and wanted to get to know him.

'So, what do you think of Manchester so far?' Steve asked.

'It's great, but a bit lonely sometimes,' Roy replied. 'It's nice to be out tonight instead of eating in my room.'

'Are your friends and family going to visit?' Robbo said.

'Try stopping them!' Roy said, laughing. 'They're

all huge United fans. Who do I talk to about getting extra tickets?'

Steve glanced at Robbo and they both grinned. 'Me!' Robbo said.

In addition, Roy spent a lot of time with Denis Irwin, who was also from Cork. They talked about home and their families, and Denis gave him the lowdown on everything a new player should know about life at United.

When the season began away to Norwich, Robbo was out injured, so Roy was thrown straight into the team, playing in midfield with Paul Ince.

'You and Incey need to run the show,' Ferguson explained in the last training session before the game. 'Make those runs and trust the other lads to find you.'

Roy loved the sound of that. He settled in quickly, and United ended their first game with a 2–0 win.

'Well played, Roy,' Ferguson said back in the dressing room. But there were no big celebrations. These kinds of results were expected at United.

Roy had soon started thinking about the next game. He wouldn't have to wait long. It was just three days away, and it would be his home debut – against Sheffield United in front of a packed crowd at Old Trafford.

The crowd cheered his name when the starting line-up was read out on the loudspeakers. Roy had goosebumps on his arms. He could see why they called Old Trafford 'The Theatre of Dreams'.

Roy was always ready to sprint onto a through ball. When a long punt forced the Sheffield United defenders to scramble back, he sensed a chance. Giggsy flicked the ball on into open space and Roy was on the move. Suddenly he was through on goal, one-on-one against the keeper.

He didn't even need to take a touch. He just calmly sent the goalie the wrong way with a low shot into the corner.

Gooooooooooooooooooooooaaaaaaaaaaaaaaaaaaa aaaaaaalllllllllllllllllllllllllllll!

As he celebrated with Giggsy and Incey, Roy looked up into the crowd of cheering fans – his new home fans. It was such a relief to score and now there would probably be less talk about his big transfer fee.

But Roy was still hungry for more scoring chances.

Mark controlled a pass just inside the penalty area, held off defenders, then slid a pass across to Roy.

Again, Roy didn't overthink it. He drilled a first-time shot before the keeper could get his positioning right and saw the net ripple.

Goooooooooooooooooooooooaaaaaaaaaaaaaaaaaaa aaaaaaalllllllllllllllllllllllllllll!

'You're just showing off now!' Steve joked.

It was the perfect home debut and a night that Roy would always remember.

In November, he got his first experience of the Manchester derby. The boos rang out loud and clear at Maine Road when Roy jogged onto the pitch with Eric and Steve for the warm-up. He had expected it at the home of Manchester City, and he knew that City would be up for this game.

On one of his trademark runs, Roy raced onto an early through ball, all alone, but his shot was saved by the keeper. He shook his head in disappointment, and he felt even worse when City took a 2–0 lead before half-time. There was a mix of shock and anger as the United players left the pitch.

Ferguson was fuming at the break, but they all knew that a lot could change in forty-five minutes. Roy looked around the dressing room and saw match-winners everywhere.

'Crank up the energy and let's see how City handle that,' Ferguson said to Roy and Giggsy.

Eric pulled a goal back after a City mistake, but the minutes flew by. In a flash, United pulled level. Eric passed to Roy, who poked the ball onto Mark. Mark set up Giggsy and his beautiful sweeping cross was perfect for Eric to tap in. Roy punched the air as he ran to celebrate with Eric.

'There's still time to win this!' Roy shouted.

With three minutes to go, Denis got the ball on the left wing and Roy was instantly sprinting into the box. Denis curled in a cross and the ball skimmed past Mark, who was battling with a City defender. Roy's eyes lit up. It was coming right to him. He stuck out his right foot, and guided the ball into the bottom corner.

Goooooooooooooooooooooaaaaaaaaaaaaaaaaaaa aaaaaaalllllllllllllllllllllllllllllll!

What a moment! Roy kept on running over to the

corner flag and slid on his stomach. His teammates rushed to pile on top of him.

'You little legend!' Steve shouted, hugging Roy. The United fans were going to love him even more now!

Every game mattered at United, but Roy had never felt fitter. With everyone playing their part, they went on to win the league, and the FA Cup too, beating Chelsea 4–0 at Wembley.

'It's nice to be on the winning team at Wembley finally!' Roy said, hugging Ferguson and Kidd and thinking back to his cup final losses at Forest.

Roy still had a lot of room to grow at United, but he couldn't have asked for a better first season. He was full of confidence as he headed into a busy summer.

CHAPTER 12

A WILD WORLD CUP: PART ONE

'What a life!' Roy said, grinning and leaning back in his seat ready for the flight to Florida, where the Ireland squad would be based during the lead-up to the 1994 World Cup.

If playing for Manchester United wasn't enough of a thrill, Roy was now heading to the World Cup with his Ireland teammates.

'My family back home still can't believe I'm going to the World Cup!' Roy told Phil Babb, another young player, during the flight.

'Yeah, it's the sort of thing I dreamed about as a kid,' Phil replied.

No one was predicting that Ireland would go far at the tournament, but Roy was confident about their chances. This squad had some quality players, with Paul McGrath in defence, and Andy Townsend and Ray Houghton in midfield.

But it was going to take some time to adjust to the conditions. It was scorching hot in Florida and Roy felt it as soon as he stepped off the plane.

'We need to get used to this heat,' manager Jack Charlton explained. 'Let's start with a few laps of the pitch.'

Roy set off quickly, jogging next to Steve and Paul. Then there were more running drills, in and out of cones and short sprints.

'We're going to be exhausted before we even get to the first game!' Steve said.

Roy wiped his sweaty face on his sleeve. He was thinking the same thing. Finally, the coaches called for a break and the balls came out. But the sun was even hotter now. Was this really the best way to prepare for the group games?

Roy took a deep breath. Seeing signs for the

World Cup in the hotel reception area, he reminded himself that he was still living the dream as a twenty-two-year-old playing in the biggest football tournament on the planet. That cheered him up a bit.

He was just counting the days until the Italy match and crossing his fingers that no one got injured in training. But even though he tried not to, Roy always compared everything to his experiences at United. Why wasn't everything just as organised with Ireland?

The squad travelled up to New York to take on Italy in their first game, and the weather was hot there too. Some of Roy's teammates even walked onto the pitch wearing baseball caps. There was no chance he was going to do that. He looked around the stadium and was surprised to see the Irish fans outnumbering the Italian fans. There was green everywhere. Roy stood next to Denis for the national anthem, wearing the Number 6 shirt and hoping that all the fans felt as fired up as he did.

There were lots of threats from Italy, but Roberto Baggio was the biggest dangerman. Roy and Paul were still talking about how to handle Baggio as they were waiting for kick-off.

'If he drops deeper into the midfield, I'll mark him,' Roy said.

'Okay, but let's keep talking during the game,' Paul suggested. 'If you need to pass him on to me, just shout.'

With the fans singing and cheering, Ireland made a dream start as Ray pounced on a loose ball and hit a dipping left-footed shot that dropped over the Italian keeper's head. 1–0!

Roy raced over, jumping onto the pile of green shirts. They really believed they could win this.

'Was that a mishit?' Roy asked.

'I don't know what you're talking about!' Ray replied with a wink.

But there was still a long way to go. Roy didn't lose his focus, intercepting passes and closing down Baggio and the other Italy attackers. That was the plan now – and it suited Roy just fine. Even in this heat, he knew he had enough energy to keep going.

Ireland first had to protect the lead and force Italy into long shots. That plan worked well. Italy fired shots over the crossbar again and again.

At last, the final whistle sounded, and the celebrations could begin, with the substitutes running onto the pitch. Roy ran to Ray, then to Denis and Steve. He saw smiling, sweaty Irish faces all around the pitch.

The mood in the dressing room was pure joy mixed with total exhaustion. Roy sat down and didn't know if he would be able to get up again.

'No matter what happens now, we'll be going back as heroes after this!' Andy said.

While the party carried on back at the hotel, Roy was thinking about the next game. Ireland could take control of the group now and avoid some of the best teams in the knockout rounds. But the Italy game was all anyone wanted to talk about.

If the Italy game had been Ireland's cup final, how would they rise to the moment against Mexico and Norway in their next two games? Roy was starting to get a bad feeling about that.

'Why can't we have higher expectations for once?' he asked Denis.

A few days later, Ireland had to do it all again as they took on Mexico.

'We're going to use our height to unsettle them,' manager Charlton explained. 'Every chance you get, whack the ball forward.'

Roy did as he was told. But he couldn't help but look around the dressing room and wonder why so many talented footballers were being told to just punt the ball forward. Just as he had feared, that plan backfired. Mexico cruised to an easy win, and Roy just shook his head as he left the pitch.

Next, Ireland went into their final group game against Norway with pressure to get at least a point. Again, the plan felt basic. The message seemed to be: just hang on for a draw.

Roy won tackles in midfield, but nothing was really clicking up front with the long ball tactic. He was just happy to get off the pitch with a 0–0 draw.

There were hugs and cheers in the dressing room, but Roy found it hard to get excited. Ireland were into the knockout rounds, but their performances were getting worse. 'We could have won the group with a different mindset,' Roy said to Denis as they were leaving the stadium.

Now they were stuck with a match against the Netherlands, who had brilliant players like Dennis Bergkamp, Ronald Koeman and the de Boer brothers. A miserable 2–0 loss sent Ireland home, but Roy was stunned on their arrival back in Ireland to see him and his teammates welcomed home like heroes. Sure, the win over Italy was special, but he had never seen so much excitement for not even reaching the quarter-finals.

Roy just hoped he would have other chances on the world stage – because it felt like Ireland had wasted a golden chance at this World Cup.

CHAPTER 13

SECOND BEST

Back at United, Roy was ready to go all out to win the big trophies, but he quickly saw that the 1994–95 season was going to be a battle, with Blackburn proving they were ready to take down the champions. The two teams were locked together at the top.

Roy loved that kind of pressure, and it brought out the fiery side of his game. That was always a difficult balance for Roy. He was at his best when he was playing with 'an edge', as one of his coaches called it. It made him a force in midfield and someone that no one enjoyed playing against.

It also landed him in trouble with referees. Roy was never afraid to fly into a tackle and have a few words with an opponent. When he lost his cool, a yellow card was never far away – and sometimes it was even worse than that.

His no-nonsense approach certainly went too far against Crystal Palace in the FA Cup semi-final that season, and he got his first red card as a United player. They still won the game, but Roy apologised to Ferguson and his teammates in the dressing room. He had lashed out – and there was no excuse.

Roy wasn't going to change the way he played, though, and it was that intensity which helped United keep chasing Blackburn.

'It doesn't get much better than this,' the TV announcer said. 'The Premier League title race comes down to the final day of the season, with just two points separating Blackburn and Manchester United.'

Blackburn were finishing the season at Anfield against Liverpool, and United were away to West Ham. Roy went through all his usual warm-up exercises, but his heart was pounding. It was hard to believe that the whole season hinged on the next ninety minutes.

'We can't control what happens in Blackburn's game,' Ferguson reminded them all. 'We've got to win first and then see if they slip up.'

When West Ham took the lead, United's chances of snatching the title looked slim, especially with the news that Blackburn were winning. But the second half brought fresh hope. United equalised, then Liverpool pulled level with Blackburn.

United threw everything at West Ham, creating chance after chance. Andy and Mark had chances saved, and another shot was blocked on the line.

Roy was subbed off for the last ten minutes, and he could hardly watch from the bench while United fired desperate long balls into the box. When the final whistle blew, Roy put his hands on his head. He felt even worse when they all found out that Blackburn had lost to a last-minute goal.

It was impossible not to think back to the games when they had struggled that season – a silly goal here, a bad miss there. Those were the tiny moments that had decided the title race. Roy wished he could go back in a time machine and replay those matches.

'I can't believe it,' he told his brothers. 'We were so close. One goal. That's all we needed.' As they talked, he could hear their own disappointment as United fans.

But there was no time to feel sorry for themselves. United were in the FA Cup final against Everton the following weekend. That gave Roy something else to think about. They could still end the season with a trophy.

Everton had finished in fifteenth place in the Premier League table that season. Looking at the two squads, it was no contest. United had the stars and the big-game experience, even with Eric suspended and Andy ruled out.

But losing the title had rocked the dressing room more than anyone wanted to admit. Though they said all the right things in the build-up to the final about moving on and focusing on the FA Cup, the spark was missing. Even the power of Wembley couldn't snap them out of it.

When Everton went ahead with a fast break goal, Roy knew it wouldn't be easy for United to dig their way out of this hole. They just couldn't score. Giggsy mishit a shot. Brian McClair's header bounced back off the bar. Young midfielder Paul Scholes's shot was well saved.

'How did he save that?' Roy said.

Every time United got near the Everton goal, there was a swarm of blue shirts blocking the way. They won a late corner and the giant goalie Peter Schmeichel rushed forward to join the crowd in the penalty area. But even that didn't work. Everton cleared the ball away and soon they were celebrating in front of their fans, while the United players were walking around in a daze. What had just happened?!

Thirty minutes later, there were still stunned faces all around the dressing room. If winning the Double in his first season was a total dream, the 1994–95 season was a harsh reminder for Roy that football could sometimes be cruel too.

'It's going to feel like a long summer,' Steve said, shaking his head and staring at the floor.

'I know it hurts, but remember this feeling,' Ferguson insisted. He looked like he was still trying to digest it all. 'We're going to come back stronger next season.'

Roy didn't know what to say. He just felt totally drained after the last two weeks. Two trophies had slipped through their fingers in the most heartbreaking way, and he was going to need some time to get over it. While he and Theresa prepared for a summer holiday in the sun, Roy hoped he would come back refreshed.

A season without a major trophy wasn't acceptable at a club like United, and he knew the pressure would be on, as they headed into the 1995–96 season.

CHAPTER 14

KEEPING UP WITH THE "KIDS"

It only took a couple of laps of the pitch in preseason training to sense a different vibe around the club. United had made some bold changes after the disappointment of the previous season. Mark and Paul Ince had left, and the message from Ferguson was clear: the 1995–96 season was going to be a fresh start.

United were looking to the future, with an incredible group of academy players desperate for their chance. Roy had heard all about them, and he had seen enough to believe the hype.

Giggsy had already been a big academy success story, and now Paul Scholes and Nicky Butt were stepping up as central midfielders. David Beckham (Becks) had a big reputation as a winger or central midfielder, and Gary and Phil Neville had emerged as promising defenders.

They had all been playing together for years in the United youth teams, and that had created great chemistry on the pitch and an inseparable bond off the pitch. But it was a big gamble in some ways. Ferguson would be asking teenagers to replace United legends.

'These younger players are unbelievable,' Roy told Theresa after the first week of preseason training. 'When I think back to when I was nineteen, I was nowhere close to their level. It might be bumpy for them at the start, but the club is in good hands.'

The United squad arrived at Villa Park for the first game of the season, with Scholes, Butt and the Nevilles all in the starting line-up, surrounded by the more experienced core of Peter, Steve, Roy, Giggsy and Eric. But that afternoon quickly turned into a disaster as they slipped to a 3–1 loss.

The youngsters were huddled together in the dressing room after the game, and they all looked a bit rattled.

'Forget about that one,' Roy told them, remembering what it was like when he first entered the United squad. 'It was a tough day for all of us. We'll be better in the next game.'

But everyone was writing United off after that result. When the highlights finished on *Match of the Day*, the verdict was harsh: 'You can't win anything with kids,' one of the experts said.

With the doubters circling around United, Roy understood that he needed to respond – but not with comments at a press conference. Anyone could do that. He would let his football do the talking.

In the first home game of the season, Roy found a yard of space against West Ham and fired a low shot into the net.

Goooooooooooooooooooooooaaaaaaaaaaaaaaaaaaa aaaaaaallllllllllllllllllllllllllll!

Three days later against Wimbledon, Roy was the hero again.

'Scholesy, I'm here!' he shouted, spotting that the defenders were out of position.

Scholesy poked through a pass and Roy did the rest,

controlling it and curling a shot past the keeper.

Goooooooooooooooooooooooaaaaaaaaaaaaaaaaaaaaaaaaaalllllllllllllllllllllllllll!

With United looking solid in defence, Roy had the freedom to push forward, and he was in the box again when the Wimbledon keeper spilled a shot. Roy got to the ball in a flash and thumped it in.

Goooooooooooooooooooooooaaaaaaaaaaaaaaaaaaaaaaaaaalllllllllllllllllllllllllll!

United hit a rough stretch in December, with Newcastle racing ahead at the top. It was a combination of too many sloppy performances and some inspired opponents. For every team, facing United was the biggest game of the season – and they played like it.

A trip to Newcastle in early March was the game that everyone had circled in the calendar. 'Think of this as a new challenge for us,' Ferguson said. 'We haven't really had to chase a team before, so let's put some pressure on them and see how they react.'

'We really need to win this one to close the gap,' Roy said, while passing the ball around the pitch with

Denis and Eric.

But United were defending desperately for most of the game. Roy tried to close down the attacks, but Newcastle came forward again and again, forcing Peter to make countless crucial saves.

'We've had some luck but it's still 0–0,' Roy said to Giggsy when they were leaving the dressing room for the second half. 'We just need one chance at the other end.'

All the defending felt worth it when Phil broke free down the left wing and his cross reached Eric at the back post. Roy was already jumping to celebrate as Eric swivelled to fire in a first-time shot.

'Get in!' Roy screamed. He knew United didn't really deserve it, but they were winning.

Roy left the pitch with a huge smile on his face. There was something extra sweet about picking up three points from a game where they really had to cling on.

That game swung the title race. As Newcastle faltered, United stormed ahead. By May, when he was holding the Premier League trophy in the air, Roy had wiped the whole of the last season from his mind.

He was still riding high as the United squad arrived at Wembley for the FA Cup final – and he could hardly believe his eyes when he saw the Liverpool team arrive in designer white suits.

'Have you seen the Liverpool suits?!' Roy asked one of the United physios.

'It's kind of hard to miss them,' Denis commented from across the room.

'Denis, promise me you'll have a word with me if you ever see me wearing something like that,' Roy said.

United weren't taking the suits seriously, but they knew Liverpool would be up for this final.

With just a few minutes to go, and with extra-time looming, it was 0–0. No problem, Roy thought. He was ready to keep battling.

United won a corner on the right wing, and Beckham jogged over to take it. All the United fans behind the goal were roaring for one last chance.

The corner was whipped in, and the Liverpool goalkeeper came flying out. But he could only push the ball away as he crashed into the sea of bodies packed into the penalty area.

Roy had drifted towards the edge of the box, and that's where the loose ball was bouncing – but not to Roy. It went to Eric instead. Without even taking a touch to control it, Eric swivelled and fired a shot from the edge of the area. It whistled through all the players and flew into the net. An incredible late winner!

Roy leapt onto the pile of celebrating teammates. Wembley was rocking.

'I don't believe it!' the commentator roared. 'You couldn't write this script!'

Back in the dressing room, the music was pumping and the players were dancing and singing.

'Another Double!' Roy called out. 'What more could I ask for?'

'One of those white suits, perhaps?' Ferguson said, walking into the room, and all the players burst into laughter.

As the 1996–97 season kicked off, United had learned their lesson. They started well, climbed to the top of the table and never looked like giving up their lead, not even with a few sloppy weeks along the way. Newcastle were still dangerous and they had signed

Alan Shearer, who picked them instead of joining United, but they weren't quite ready.

'We've always got an extra gear in Premier League games,' Roy said, discussing the latest win with his family. 'But I wish we used it more often. If we did, maybe it would carry over when we play in Europe.'

He was proved right a few weeks later when United fell short in the Champions League semi-finals. All the same, it still felt great to win another Premier League title. That was his third in four seasons at United, and he was still just as hungry to win more.

Roy was playing well, and feeling settled in Manchester. Best of all, he and Theresa got married that summer. He had never been happier.

CHAPTER 15

CAPTAIN KEANO AND A LOST SEASON

'I thought this preseason might be a bit quieter after all of last summer's transfers,' Roy said, sitting in the cafeteria with Giggsy and Denis. 'But I guess not!'

Eric had caught a lot of people by surprise by announcing his retirement after one last title party, and it was hard to imagine life at United without him. But Roy knew their only choice was to keep going.

It was the run-up to the 1997–98 season. As the players went through some drills, in preparation for their first preseason game, the assistant manager Brian Kidd called Roy over.

'The boss wants to see you in his office before you

go,' he said, with a face that gave nothing away.

Roy's mind whirled through the last few days, but he couldn't think of why Ferguson would want a meeting. 'Sure,' he replied.

After showering and changing, he took the stairs up to the manager's office.

'Don't worry, I won't drag this out, but it's important,' Ferguson said, with a grin. 'There's been a lot of change around here over the past few years. But we've still got some great leaders to rely on and, with Eric leaving, we need a new captain. I want him to be you, Roy.'

Roy smiled. He had loved the club ever since signing four years ago. He knew the history – there had been some incredible United captains over the years, including Robbo, Steve and Eric – and understood this was a huge honour.

'Thanks, boss,' he replied, shaking hands. 'That means a lot.'

He and Ferguson had spent enough time together to understand there was no chance of Roy bursting into happy tears or jumping around his office, but it was still a big moment and they both knew it.

Roy had already captained the team a few times, but it felt different to be given the armband officially. Leading the team out, away to Tottenham on the opening weekend of the new season, he was very aware of the extra responsibility on his shoulders now. One by one, the more experienced players had moved on from United, and now Roy was one of the most senior voices in the dressing room.

He got an even bigger jolt of excitement in his first home game as captain. Hearing the crowd chanting 'Keano! Keano! Keano!', Roy waved and clapped.

But his season was about to be turned upside down. Facing Leeds in a particularly physical game, Roy tried to keep his cool. The Leeds players had been flying into tackles all afternoon and it was like they were begging Roy to lash out.

Again and again, Roy just cleared the ball and ignored it. Then in the final minutes, with United losing 1–0, he chased a long pass. As he stretched to reach it, he heard a pop in his knee and crumpled to the floor.

'Argh!' he yelled, lying face down on the pitch.

A few of the Leeds players thought he was faking. They shouted at Roy, telling him to get up, but he couldn't. His teammates rushed over.

'Oh no!' Denis said when he saw the pain all over Roy's face. He had never seen his teammate on the ground unless it was something serious.

Roy hobbled back down the tunnel, and he could see the worry on the physio's face as he looked at his knee. Even the tiniest movement sent a heat wave of pain up his leg, and it was even more swollen the following day.

The United doctors confirmed the bad news. Roy had suffered serious ligament damage in his knee. Just like that, his season was over and all the dreams for his first season as captain were crushed. He was given strict instructions about resting, but it only took a few hours before he got bored of sitting on the sofa.

'It's hard to feel part of the team and bring the authority as captain when I'm just a spectator every week,' he told his parents. He just tried to help where he could when other players stepped into bigger roles – maybe a word of advice for a youngster or a tactical suggestion from the last game.

What else could he do? The physios worked with him every week, and he gradually moved on to exercises in the gym and the swimming pool. Some days, his knee felt much improved, but he understood there was no point in rushing his return and having to start all over again. Patience was the key – and that was never Roy's biggest strength.

Without him, United lost the title race to Arsenal by one point. There would be no third championship in a row, but Roy often thought about how things might have been different if he hadn't missed so many weeks.

As he sat down at the nearest gym machine to continue his latest workout, he took a breath and adjusted the weights. This had felt like a lost season, but he promised himself that he would make up for it next year.

CHAPTER 16

THE TREBLE

With his knee fully healed, Roy had big targets for the 1998–99 season – and that meant chasing every single trophy.

By the time the calendar had flipped round to April, United were top of the Premier League table, and into the semi-finals of the FA Cup and Champions League. Everywhere Roy looked, someone was talking about their chances of winning the 'Treble'.

The Champions League was always the missing piece of the puzzle. When Roy thought about the previous five seasons and all of United's spectacular achievements, European glory had slipped through their fingers again and again.

Arriving at the hotel before their Champions League

semi-final second leg against Juventus, Roy was determined to avoid the same old story.

'If we're going to finally break through in Europe, this is the team to do it,' Roy had told his brothers at the weekend.

It was easy to see why Roy thought that. This United squad had everything. Andy Cole and new signing Dwight Yorke had become a deadly strikeforce, with Ole Gunnar Solskjaer and Teddy Sheringham also banging in the goals. Giggsy and Becks created chance after chance on the wings, Roy was tireless in midfield and giant Jaap Stam had made the defence even stronger.

Still, United had never reached a Champions League final during Roy's time at the club – or during Ferguson's years in charge. To get there, they would need the performance of their lives against Juventus. The first leg had finished 1–1, but United were short of their best. Now this second leg was set up perfectly to be a classic.

They had gone over the game plan in detail countless times – in training and in the hotel meeting room. But United still made a nightmare start. After just eleven minutes, Juventus were 2–0 up, and breezing towards the final.

Roy took a second to digest it all. United were on the ropes, but there was no point yelling and screaming. They needed to regroup and calm down.

'Come on, lads!' he called. 'Keep your heads up. There's still a lot of football left to be played here.'

Channelling his past golden performance for Cobh Ramblers when the game seemed to have slipped away, Roy went into turbo mode. He was everywhere, winning tackles, intercepting passes and urging the team forward. He didn't have to say much – he just led by example and pulled everyone along with him.

United won a corner and Becks jogged over to take it.

'We've got to make these chances count,' Roy muttered to himself while he waited in the penalty area.

As Becks swung in the corner, Roy set off on a near post run and got a step ahead of his marker. The ball fizzed towards him. In an instant, he knew he only needed a slight touch. Becks's crosses always had so much whip on them, so Roy just focused on making contact and glancing a header towards the goal.

He timed his jump perfectly and watched the ball fly past the keeper and into the net.

Goooooooooooooooooooooooaaaaaaaaaaaaaaaaaaa aaaaaaalllllllllllllllllllllllllllll!

United were back in business.

'Get in!' he shouted, while Becks sprinted over to celebrate.

Now Roy was really in the zone. He sensed Juventus fading and he was winning the midfield battle against Zinedine Zidane and Edgar Davids. As Zidane tried to twist away, Roy lunged to reach the ball. But this time, he was a second too late. He tripped Zidane and turned in horror to see the referee holding up a yellow card.

Roy looked at the ground and shook his head. He couldn't believe it. This latest yellow card meant he would be suspended for the Champions League final if United made it there.

Some players would have let the disappointment take them out of the game, but Roy brushed it off. He could think about that later. He had a game to win, and he wasn't going to ease off.

Instead, he ran even harder, rallying his teammates.

'Gary, play it up the line.'

'Becks, I'm just inside, lay it off.'

'Jaap, watch out for the striker behind you.'

Before half-time, United equalised. Andy set up Dwight, who thumped a header into the net. They were now ahead on away goals, which would be the decider if the scores were level on aggregate.

As Juventus pushed for a goal, Dwight raced clear on a counterattack. He collided with the goalkeeper, but Andy was there to slide in the rebound. What a comeback!

Roy had a big smile on his face at full-time, as the United players celebrated an incredible fightback. Then the reality hit him like running into a brick wall. In the frenzy of the comeback, he had almost forgotten that he would be suspended for the final.

'In all these years together, that's the best game I've ever seen you play,' Ferguson said, putting a hand on Roy's shoulder. 'It was an honour to be your manager tonight. The suspension is so cruel, but you led us to the final. Don't ever forget that.'

The Treble was still on, but it was also possible for

United to finish with nothing.

'Just win three games in ten days,' Becks said, with a big smile. 'That's all we've got to do.'

'Well, thanks, Becks,' Roy replied. 'It sounds so simple when you put it like that.'

The first job was to clinch the Premier League title. A win against Tottenham on the final day would make United champions. But if they drew and Arsenal won, the trophy would stay at Highbury.

Roy thought back to 1995 and the agony of losing the title race away to West Ham. 'We can't go through that again,' he said to Giggsy as they warmed up.

But there were some scary moments ahead. Tottenham went 1–0 up, then Becks scored just before half-time. United still needed another goal, though.

'Throw everything at them for the next fifteen minutes,' Ferguson said at half-time. 'But play together. No one should be trying to do it on their own.'

'One goal, that's all we need,' Roy added.

It only took a few minutes. Andy's perfect lob made it 2–1 and United held on. They were champions again! Ferguson wrapped Roy in a hug while the Old

Trafford crowd stayed to applaud their lap of honour.

One down, two to go.

Roy was fired up for the FA Cup final. For him, this was the last game of the season, and he was going to give it his all. Unfortunately, his ankle was already sore, and a late tackle made it even worse. Roy limped off, but United went on to win 2–0.

Now came the hard part. Roy travelled to Barcelona with the rest of the squad and went to the meetings, but he could only watch from the bench in a grey suit when matchday arrived. Scholesy was also suspended and they sat together, both feeling the pain of missing the biggest game of the season.

United missed him too. They went 1–0 down, and Roy could see it was the type of game where he would up the tempo and force everyone to find extra energy.

'Come on,' Roy whispered to himself. 'Keep fighting!'

The last few minutes were some of the wildest Roy had ever seen. Becks's corner was cleared to the edge of the box. Giggsy fired the ball back through a crowd of players and Teddy hit a first-time shot into the net.

'Yes!' Roy yelled.

United had left it late, but they were still alive.

Then they won another corner. Roy looked at Scholesy next to him on the bench. Maybe there was still time for one last chance.

'Surely we couldn't snatch it, could we?' Roy said.

Becks's corner was flicked on at the near post and Ole stuck out his feet to prod the ball into the net.

They all leapt up. Roy's head was spinning so much that it took a few minutes to realise that they had just won the Champions League. He joined his teammates on the pitch to celebrate with the fans, putting aside the strange feeling of not being part of the final.

When United got back to Manchester, there were people everywhere for the special parade that the club had arranged. No one wanted to miss out on a glimpse of the Treble winners. As the parade bus moved slowly through the streets, Roy savoured the fact that United had made history.

CHAPTER 17

CRUISING

Winning the Treble had put Manchester United among the most successful teams in football history. Roy and his teammates had set themselves big targets and they had reached them all.

'So, what's left for you to do now?' Pat asked that summer, when the Treble celebrations finally quietened down and life got back to normal.

'We go and win it all again,' he answered.

But that question stuck in Roy's mind as the United squad prepared for the 1999–2000 season, and he was sure that Ferguson had been thinking about it too.

It would be so easy for standards to drop after reaching the top. Would there be a little less hunger to win the biggest trophies when they had all the medals at home? Roy could always find new challenges to stay focused on winning, but would his teammates think the same way?

It wasn't Roy's style to give a big speech about the need to stay ready and be at their best, but he was determined to start the season well and show that there would be no complacency after all the highlights of the previous season.

An early-season trip to Highbury to take on Arsenal was a perfect opportunity to send a message. Arsenal had chased United all the way last season, finishing just one point behind.

'Let's remind them this is still our trophy and it's not going anywhere,' Roy said as the players high-fived and headed for the tunnel.

It was reassuring to look around the pitch and see all the usual faces. He had played with Giggsy, Becks and Scholesy in midfield for years, and they had a great understanding with Dwight and Andy up front.

From the first crunching tackle in midfield, Roy could tell that Arsenal were up for this, and he could imagine how he would have felt as an Arsenal player after months of hearing about their rivals' famous 'Treble'.

Arsenal went 1–0 up just before half-time and their fans were loving it, jeering and cheering every bad United pass.

There was no panic in the United dressing room, though. They weren't shouting or screaming. They just took a breath and talked through a few small adjustments to the game plan.

'We're playing well,' Ferguson said. 'Be patient and the chances will come.'

One of the adjustments for the second half was for Roy and Scholesy to take turns making runs from midfield to give Dwight and Andy support. Roy had been more cautious in the first half, sticking close to Patrick Vieira.

Now United needed more from him. The ball bounced up in midfield, and Scholesy and Vieira went for it. In the scramble, Scholesy poked a pass to Roy.

Roy could see that Arsenal were out of position. He played a first-time pass to Andy and then kept running, seeing a gap behind the defence.

'Slide it through!' he shouted, pointing for where he wanted the pass.

Andy spotted him and put the ball right onto Roy's foot. He didn't even have to slow down. He just placed a shot under the goalkeeper's dive and saw the ball roll into the bottom corner.

Goooooooooooooooooooooooaaaaaaaaaaaaaaaaaaaa aaaaaaalllllllllllllllllllllllllllll!

'Get in!' he yelled as he ran over to celebrate near the United fans.

Arsenal looked rattled. Vieira grabbed at Roy, who stood his ground, even though he was much shorter. 'What are you doing?' Roy asked, glaring.

With just a few minutes to go, Giggsy won the ball back in midfield, swiping it away from an Arsenal player. Again, Roy saw a chance to get into the box. He sprinted forward and saw Giggsy lining up a shot. Roy didn't wait to see where the shot went. He carried on running in case the keeper spilled out a rebound.

But the ball didn't reach the keeper. Giggsy's shot deflected off an Arsenal leg and floated up in front of Roy. He controlled the ball on his chest and calmly flicked a shot with the outside of his right foot. Almost in slow motion, the ball dropped into the net.

Goooooooooooooooooooooooaaaaaaaaaaaaaaaaaa aaaaaaalllllllllllllllllllllllllll!

Roy ran off to celebrate again, dodging one way then the other to escape his teammates. Eventually they caught up with him, burying him in hugs.

'You'll be our new striker if you keep this up!' Dwight said, laughing.

United clung on for a 2–1 win and Roy walked off the pitch feeling ten feet tall. It wasn't just about the goals. He was more excited about beating one of United's toughest rivals and keeping up the winning habits. That performance also strengthened his case for a big new contract.

United cruised through the next few months and strolled to their second straight title, finishing eighteen points ahead of Arsenal, who were second. Some of Roy's fears came true in the Champions League, though. United just weren't quite as sharp as the other top European teams and they lost to Real Madrid in the quarter-finals. Not for the first time, Roy wondered whether their easy ride in the Premier League had hidden some of their weaknesses – and he knew that a few of his red cards had been sparked by his frustration that United's standards didn't seem quite as high.

The 2000–01 season was a similar story; again, United dominated the league but stumbled in Europe. There were still some magical performances, though, including a 6–1 win over Arsenal at Old Trafford.

During that Arsenal game, Dwight smashed a quickfire hat-trick and then Roy gave himself more freedom to get forward. As Dwight ran clear again down the left wing, he cut inside, just as Roy was making his run. He was a step ahead of the nearest defender.

In a flash, Dwight floated the ball towards the back post. Roy took a touch to control it and then thumped a shot into the bottom corner before the keeper could react.

Goooooooooooooooooooooooaaaaaaaaaaaaaaaaaaaa aaaaaaalllllllllllllllllllllllllllll!

Roy still had a nagging feeling that United weren't quite as good as the Premier League table suggested, but a third straight title was a special achievement.

It was the 2001–02 season, though, that really emphasised United's weaknesses. Arsenal took the

Premier League trophy back, clinching it with a 1–0 win at Old Trafford.

'I'm not even that surprised,' Roy told Theresa. 'We've been slipping for the last few seasons.'

United saved some of their best performances for the Champions League that year. Roy had missed some of the group games with a hamstring injury, but he was back in time for the semi-final second leg against German club Bayer Leverkusen. The first leg had finished in a disappointing 2–2 draw, so United would probably need to win in Germany now.

Roy was fired up, leading the team out. He knew what this meant. After missing the 1999 Champions League final, he was just ninety minutes away from getting a second chance to play in a big European final.

In one first-half attack, he ended up further forward than usual, but he kept going when Ruud van Nistelrooy dribbled forward. Ruud's pass bobbled behind the defence, giving Roy the clearest path. He took a touch to go around the keeper and then carefully dinked a shot into the net from a tight angle with his left foot.

'Let's do this!' he shouted, running off to celebrate. United were a step closer to the final.

But Leverkusen hit back, earning a 1–1 draw that sent United out on away goals. Roy felt numb at full-time while the home fans cheered in delight. No one needed to remind him that this may have been his last chance to reach a Champions League final.

It hadn't been a memorable year for United, but at least it was a big one for Ireland. With Roy leading the way in midfield, Ireland qualified for the 2002 World Cup, finishing level on points with Portugal and ahead of the Netherlands. That put Ireland into a playoff where they edged past Iran.

'Nobody outside our dressing room thought we could make it to the World Cup,' Roy told his kids. He smiled as he thought about some of the wins, including an exhausting 1–0 victory against the Netherlands, with only ten men.

Roy was still simmering about some of the issues at United, but for now, he had to focus on a big summer ahead with Ireland.

CHAPTER 18

A WILD WORLD CUP: PART TWO

'Are they still there?' Roy asked Theresa, fidgeting in his chair.

She walked over to the window and moved the curtains an inch to peek outside.

'Yes, most of them are,' she said, sounding a mixture of sad and annoyed. 'There are a couple of cameramen by the gate, and I can see reporters huddled around a van.'

Roy groaned. The past week had felt like a month. It was hard to believe that he had been at the 2002 World Cup in Japan only three days earlier, before this nightmare began.

The memories came flooding back. First came the happier ones: arriving at the hotel, feeling the buzz of the World Cup again and seeing the excitement for the younger players in the squad. The Irish fans were arriving at the tournament and making it a party.

Then came the steadily worse ones, like the issues with the preparation, the training pitch, the disagreements and the one blazing argument with Ireland manager Mick McCarthy that led to Roy leaving the World Cup before it had even started. He hadn't held back in the dispute with McCarthy, making his point loudly and angrily in front of the whole Ireland squad and leaving the room to stunned silence.

Roy had tried to ignore all the little problems. He really had. But he was so tired of dealing with the poor planning and unnecessary mistakes. At the first practice session, the pitch had been as hard as concrete, and a few of the players had limped off to see the physio. The balls and training kit still hadn't arrived. Roy didn't know whether to laugh or cry.

'You can't win without setting high standards,' he had thought to himself when he was back in the peace of his hotel room.

It was especially hard to take because Ireland had a really talented squad and, just as in 1994, Roy thought they could shock some of the favourites at the tournament. They could count on experienced Premier League players, and they had matched some of the top teams in the world over the past year.

But nothing had been going right, and Roy felt he had to speak up. He understood that no one else probably would, and he couldn't blame them. No one wanted to ruin their chances of playing in a World Cup by siding with Roy. So, he left, and they stayed.

'It's the World Cup,' Roy told Theresa, still feeling the frustration rising up inside him. 'We worked so hard to qualify. We had talked about how important it was to get the preparation right and take it seriously like all the other countries do, and . . .'

Roy trailed off and went silent again. Theresa just sat next to him and let him talk. She knew how hard this was for him. He loved being Irish and representing his country. That was where so much of this passion came from – he desperately wanted the team to do well.

But now Roy had become the big news story, and there was plenty of criticism about his decision to leave. The phone was ringing non-stop, but he ignored most of the calls. He spoke to his agent and to Ferguson, but he shut himself off from almost everyone else, even after getting some nice messages from his teammates.

'Try to put all of that behind you now,' Ferguson told him. 'Throw your energy into next season. We're all here for you.'

All the attention made everything worse. From his earliest days at Forest and throughout the glory years at United, Roy had found it really hard to accept that nothing about his life could be private anymore. He was usually happy to sign autographs or meet fans, but there never seemed to be any limits for what people expected from him.

It was bad enough when that meant trouble from strangers or reporters on nights out with his friends and teammates. But this obsession with him after the World Cup was on a whole new level. It was affecting him, and it was affecting his family. Surely people could see that?

Roy couldn't even face watching the matches on TV. It was still too fresh. It had been such a huge achievement for Ireland to reach this particular World Cup, after failing to qualify for the 1998 World Cup or Euro 2000. But that was all over for him now, and he realised that this might have been his last chance to play at a big tournament.

Since flying home, the world had closed in around him, with reporters lurking everywhere. It gave Roy more time to think than he really wanted, and he had decided that he wasn't going to let all the attention trap him inside.

When the restlessness of staying inside the house became too much, he called to his dog, Triggs, and they headed for the front door.

'Time for a walk,' he said, putting on his shoes.

Leaving the house, Roy was ready for the camera flashes. He and Triggs just marched past the pack of reporters and kept going down the street.

CHAPTER 19

ON TOP OF THE MOUNTAIN AGAIN

Roy felt excitement and relief as he drove into the car park at the United training ground. There was always something comforting about focusing on his football and blocking out all of the noise around him.

Leaving his stormy summer with Ireland behind, Roy was fresh and ready to put in the hard work during preseason. All eyes were on United. How would they respond after losing the title to Arsenal?

'It's back to business now, lads,' Ferguson said when he had the whole squad together. 'None of us liked the way that last season ended, so go out there and put things right.'

The previous summer, 2001, United had signed star striker Ruud van Nistelrooy and midfielder Juan Sebastián Verón, and they added Rio Ferdinand before this new 2002–03 season. But Roy knew that it was the veteran core – him, Giggsy, Scholesy, Gary, Becks – that would need to lead the way.

That still didn't stop Roy from getting in trouble within weeks, though. Once again, his temper got the better of him. A suspension, followed by surgery on his hip, kept him off the pitch and watching from the stands.

'When am I going to learn?!' he asked Theresa, thinking back to the different moments over the years where he had lost his temper during a game. 'As the captain, I should know better.'

'Yeah, Daddy, red cards are naughty!' his daughter said, running into the room with one of her toys.

When Roy returned to the team, he kickstarted an eleven-game unbeaten run. Roy's presence on the pitch seemed to inspire all of his teammates to bring a little extra focus and a little extra energy. No one wanted to have a bad game in front of Roy.

As the title race heated up in March and April, it was another head-to-head battle between United and Arsenal. This time, Roy could sense United finding their best form when it mattered most.

After falling behind, away to Newcastle, he settled things down. It was nothing fancy, but he started getting the ball to United's best attackers in dangerous areas – and they did the rest.

Ole equalised, Scholesy smashed in two screamers and every attacking move looked like a possible goal. Roy could just sit back and admire it all. Giggsy crashed in another, and it was 4–1 at half-time.

'This is football from another planet,' Roy said, high-fiving Scholesy as they headed for the tunnel. 'That's the best half I can remember playing in.'

Goals kept coming, and United rolled to a 6–2 win.

'We played like champions today,' Roy said to Ole as they sat down on the team bus.

Ole grinned. 'At one stage, I thought we might score ten,' he added.

But the biggest game was still to come – a trip to face Arsenal in a game most people were calling a title decider. These were the games that Roy lived for, and United had to dig deep in an end-to-end 2–2 draw.

As Roy went over to applaud the United fans in the far corner of the stadium, his body was aching, but he felt good about the result. Arsenal were going to have to be perfect in their final four games to catch United.

'Great performance, lads,' Roy said back in the dressing room. 'We haven't won anything yet, but I loved the character we showed tonight.'

Giggsy and Gary nodded. They all knew that nothing was guaranteed until the trophy was in their hands, but there was a definite buzz in the air. Ferguson had even come onto the pitch at the end to shake hands with each player.

Wins over Blackburn, Tottenham and Charlton put United in a great position, but Roy knew this could be leading to another dramatic final day of the season.

'I'm getting too old for all this stress,' he told Ruud, laughing. 'If the title gets decided on goal difference, I might just have to retire on the spot.'

But when Arsenal lost to Leeds, United were crowned as champions with a game to spare.

'There you go, Roy,' Ruud said at the next training session. 'You can sleep like a baby now.'

Thankfully, the United players could now relax and enjoy the last game of the season away to Everton. After a 2–1 win, Roy was standing in the tunnel, waiting for the presentation ceremony, when he spotted the Premier League trophy being carried onto the pitch. There it was, shining in the evening sun. For some of his teammates, this would be their first title, and that just added to the bubbling excitement all around him.

'We've got our trophy back!' they all sang, huddling behind a sign with the words '2002–03 Premier League Champions' on the front.

Everyone was in a party mood that night, and Roy took a moment to high-five each of his teammates. It had been a rollercoaster season, and they had all played a part in wrestling the title back from Arsenal.

When Roy had the trophy in his hands, he paused just for a second to soak in the moment. Then he raised it into the air, with his teammates cheering behind him. United were champions again!

CHAPTER 20

A NEW ROLE

Roy was used to changes at United by now, and he saw that he would have to adapt his own game if he was going to keep playing ninety minutes at this level.

When he looked back on his early years at Old Trafford, he had forgotten all the goals he used to score. But he wasn't a box-to-box midfielder anymore – and he was fine with that.

Now, his role was to start the attacks, protect the defence and control the pace of the game. He was still one of the best in the world at doing those things, as long as he stayed out of trouble with the referee.

But his major knee injury and a painful hip issue had slowed him down, and all the games and all the minutes added up. He felt like 'the old guy' in the dressing room and, with a growing family at home, he could feel the grey hairs on the way.

That summer, United turned to younger signings, starting with a flashy winger called Cristiano Ronaldo. He was joined by Klebérson and Eric Djemba-Djemba, who were talented players with exciting futures.

But Roy soon saw that it would take some time before they could really help the club win trophies.

After a slow start, United fell behind Arsenal and could only watch as Thierry Henry and the Gunners powered ahead. Almost a year after lifting the Premier League trophy at Goodison Park, the mood in the United dressing room was very different. The title race was over.

'Do you think Arsenal are going to finish unbeaten?' Giggsy asked. The question now wasn't if Arsenal would win the title – that now seemed certain – but whether they could go the whole league season undefeated.

Roy nodded. 'Yeah, I think so, they've come too far to blow it now,' he answered, sounding as disappointed as he felt. United had lost nine league games and never stood a chance.

He turned off the TV. Training was about to start, and he had heard enough about Arsenal's amazing season.

But it wasn't all doom and gloom at Old Trafford. United had still reached the FA Cup final and everyone expected them to beat Millwall. As Roy led the team out at Wembley, he could forget about the rest of the season for a few hours and enjoy this moment.

He almost scored with an early dipping shot, putting his hands on his head as the Millwall keeper tipped it over the bar. Sensing that a goal was coming, Roy kept pushing United forward. Just before half-time, he sent a pass out to Gary on the right wing. Gary whipped in a dangerous cross and Cristiano rose to head the ball in. 1–0.

Ruud scored twice in the second half to seal the win, and the party began. Roy stepped up to receive the trophy, raising it into the air as red fireworks erupted behind him.

It was nice to finish on a high note, but Roy knew that FA Cup success couldn't cover up a disappointing season. United just weren't good enough or consistent enough to stay in the Premier League title race.

Roy still had his doubts about the squad at the start of the 2004–05 season. United had signed teenage sensation Wayne Rooney, but there were so many young players who were still learning what it meant to be at their best in every game.

It felt a long way from the dressing room of leaders that he had been used to at the club, and Roy sensed it wasn't going to be easy to wrestle the Premier League trophy back to Manchester.

Chelsea were ready to challenge after spending big money in the transfer market and they were soon piling up wins. But nothing could top the United-Arsenal clashes, and Roy produced an outstanding captain's performance in a fiery 4–2 win at Highbury.

There just wasn't enough consistency across the whole team, though. For the second year in a row, United couldn't keep pace in the Premier League and had to settle for a good cup run instead.

In the FA Cup quarter-final against Southampton, Roy even reminded his teammates that he could still pop up with the occasional goal. He received the ball under pressure but created half a yard of space as he twisted away from his marker. That set him up perfectly for a shot with his right foot and he hammered a wonder strike past the keeper.

Goooooooooooooooooooooooaaaaaaaaaaaaaaaaaaaa aaaaaaalllllllllllllllllllllllllllll!

Scholesy and Wayne ran over to celebrate with him.

'Why do you all look so surprised?' Roy said, with a grin. 'I used to score all the time when I was younger!'

United made it back to the FA Cup final for another instalment of their rivalry with Arsenal, and it was especially heated after another argument between Roy and Vieira in the last game. A trip to Wembley was always a special occasion, but Roy and his teammates were left to regret some missed chances after the game finished 0–0 and went to penalties.

By the time it was Roy's turn, Scholesy's penalty had already been saved. Roy had to score to keep United's hopes alive. With the rain hammering down on him, he took his time and calmly placed it past the keeper.

But Vieira won it for Arsenal with the next penalty, leaving Roy and United empty-handed. As the players headed off for their summer holidays, there were questions hanging in the air.

How could United close the gap in the Premier League? For how much longer would the older players like Roy and Giggsy be around? Who would United sign before next season?

Even with exciting young players like Cristiano and Wayne around, Roy knew there was still a lot of work to do.

CHAPTER 21

LEAVING UNITED, CHOOSING CELTIC

During his twelve years at the club, Roy had become a United legend, and he ranked among the greatest players to ever wear the famous red shirt. But all good things must come to an end, and the 2005–06 season turned out to be his last at Old Trafford.

Tensions were building all year. On the pitch, United were still searching for more consistency. Off the pitch, it was the last year of Roy's contract, and that created more uncertainty about his future.

Then Roy broke his foot, and he found himself spending more time with the doctors and physios than with his teammates. As much as he disliked being a helpless spectator, it gave Roy another chance to assess the team's strengths and weaknesses.

And Roy didn't like what he saw. A 4–1 loss against Middlesbrough was the lowest point, and there was nothing he could do about it. He had been part of so many great United teams, full of winners who worked hard and were hungry to improve every day. Were the current players going to reach that level?

Roy had never been afraid to share his opinions on where the team needed to improve, and he was trying to be patient as young players settled in. But he also believed that pushing them harder was part of his job as a captain and a leader.

That led to arguments with Ferguson and assistant manager Carlos Queiroz. Eventually, he was called to a meeting with Ferguson and United's chairman David Gill.

'We've come to the end, Roy,' they said. 'We're going to be ending your contract, and here's a statement that we're going to release.'

Roy had reached the end too. If that was how they felt, he would go.

After all the years and all the trophies, it was a sad way to say goodbye to Manchester United. During his drive home, his head was still juggling all the different emotions. He felt angry, sad and confused all at the same time.

Finally, when he put all those feelings aside, Roy thought about what he wanted to do next, and he sat at home for a few days.

'Do you still want to play?' Theresa asked as she and Roy sat in the kitchen.

That was the question that they had been debating lately. Lots of teams were wondering the same thing and had been calling Roy's agent with offers.

'I'm not going to play for another Premier League team,' Roy said. 'That wouldn't feel right. So we could think about one of the big clubs in Spain or Germany – or there's Celtic.'

The chance to go to Celtic had taken Roy by surprise, but it was now near the top of his list. Real Madrid was another attractive option, with the history of the club and the chance to experience life in Spain.

'I want to play at least one more season,' Roy said

eventually. 'Then that's it for me.'

In the end, he picked Celtic. He liked the idea of playing for the club and it was a less disruptive move for the family.

'It's a great move for me,' he explained at his first press conference in Scotland. 'I feel that this is where I belong and I'm here to work hard and win games.'

Posing for photos holding the Celtic shirt with his number 16 on the back, he felt he had made the right decision. The bigger challenge was getting back to full fitness. After breaking his foot and going through the recovery process, he had been without a club for a few weeks and he knew he would need some training sessions to get up to speed again.

It was a boost just to join in the training sessions and start building a connection with the other players. Manager Gordon Strachan urged him not to rush his return, but there was a buzz in the air during Roy's preparations for his first game at Hampden Park.

Roy knew a lot of people back in Cork who loved Celtic, and the club had made an instant impression on him. He felt goosebumps on his arms as he walked onto the pitch for his home debut against Kilmarnock, and there was such a loud roar for his first touch.

Now he just wanted to contribute. As Celtic took on Falkirk, Roy was feeling more like his old self. When a free kick was cleared towards him, he didn't hesitate, firing a shot from just outside the box and watching in delight as it flew into the net via a slight deflection.

Goooooooooooooooooooooooaaaaaaaaaaaaaaaaaaa aaaaaaalllllllllllllllllllllllllllll!

Less than a week later, he had his first taste of the Celtic vs Rangers Old Firm Derby. Roy got lots of boos from the Rangers fans, but he had a smile on his face at the final whistle when Celtic grabbed a 1–0 win.

Roy added to his trophy cabinet, with Celtic winning the league and the Scottish League Cup, but then troublesome injuries left him hobbling again. He knew it was a sign that retirement was calling. After an incredible career as a player, Roy had walked off the pitch for the last time.

CHAPTER 22

THE NEW BOSS

While he adjusted to the first few days of retirement, Roy was starting to think about all the time he would spend with Theresa and the kids, and all the long walks he would go on with Triggs. That sounded amazing, after so many years focusing on training and games.

Then he got a phone call from former Ireland teammate Niall Quinn, with an offer that was so good he couldn't turn it down.

Though he and Roy might not ever agree about the drama that had unfolded in the 2002 World Cup, Niall had spent enough time with Roy to know that he was a leader and a winner.

Niall had taken over as chairman at Sunderland and he had stepped in as temporary manager while the club looked for a new boss. But after five straight losses to start the 2006–07 season, Niall was in a panic.

He needed a strong personality for the job – and he wanted Roy.

Roy's first reaction was to say no. He was looking forward to a break and he hadn't really thought much about becoming a coach or a manager. Part of him wondered how he would cope with watching games from the touchline without being able to impact the game himself.

But maybe this was the ideal next challenge that Roy was looking for. He liked everything he heard from Niall and asked for some time to talk it over with his family.

The more he thought about it, the more excited he got. Theresa could sense it too. 'If the Sunderland job feels right, we'll make it work,' she told him.

Later that week, Roy called Niall back. 'I'm in!' he said.

After that, everything happened in a hurry. Sunderland needed to move fast, and Roy had to figure out how to turn the team around without any preseason time to prepare.

'The fact that one of the most influential figures in world football is willing to come here should make all the Sunderland fans very happy,' Quinn said at the press conference to announce Roy as the new manager.

'All I ever expected from my teammates was one hundred per cent,' Roy added. 'I spoke to the players this morning and said if they give one hundred per cent to Sunderland there won't be a problem.'

Roy's first task was to sign a few players who would fit with his plans. He went through a few options and started making calls.

He began with some of his Old Trafford connections. Dwight agreed to join. So did Liam Miller, who had played with Roy at United. Lastly, Roy added in some extra options in defence and attack.

'That feels like pretty good business,' Niall said, holding a sheet of paper with the strengthened Sunderland squad on it.

Roy nodded. There was enough quality there to pull the team away from the relegation zone.

'You can already see the players standing an inch or two taller since you got here,' Niall added. 'They're all fired up to get to play for you.'

Now it was up to Roy to inspire this squad, using everything he had learned over the years. But there was no magic wand. Fitness work was high on his list once he took over training sessions, but he also drilled the team on the importance of grit and character. He wanted winners on the pitch.

The improvement was already obvious in practices over the next few weeks, but even Roy was a little stunned by Sunderland's climb up the table. Three quick wins settled the nerves in the dressing room, and gutsy wins in November and December powered them into the top half.

A few months earlier, Roy had been thinking about what it would take for the team to avoid relegation. Now he was dreaming bigger.

'Wow, being a manager looks really easy,' Pat teased when they spoke on the phone. 'Can anyone just start doing this now?'

'Trust me, it didn't seem easy at the start!' Roy admitted to his brother. 'But I'm starting to really enjoy it now.'

Not that he was going to ease off just because Sunderland had put together a few wins. He kept the standards high – Roy was never going to allow anything less than that – and he could see the team starting to believe they could get a result even when they weren't playing well.

Heading into April, Sunderland still hadn't lost a league game in 2007. Remarkably, they were now a serious contender to win the league.

But trailing 1–0 at Southampton, Roy turned to his subs to shake things up.

'Push forward and support the strikers,' he told Grant Leadbitter, who was standing next to him on the touchline ready to come on in midfield. 'We've still got time, so we don't need to be hoofing the ball into the box. Get it out wide. That's where we're going to create the chances.'

This was going to be the ultimate test of what he had been teaching his players all year. They had to keep believing. They had to dig even deeper to get back into the game.

Carlos Edwards, one of Sunderland's mid-season

signings, provided the first moment of magic, firing in a brilliant equaliser.

Roy was standing on the touchline again, signalling for his players to keep attacking.

With three minutes to go, Grant made the kind of run that Roy used to make in his early United years. He took a layoff onto his right foot and rocketed a shot past the Southampton keeper.

Roy clenched his fists in celebration. 'Get in!' he shouted.

'We're top of the league!' one of his coaches said as they walked back to the dressing room.

'I'm going to say the same thing I've been saying all year,' Roy told his players as they enjoyed the glow of the late winner. 'Don't look too far ahead. Just get ready for the next game.'

A 2–1 win at Birmingham City meant they had almost completed the most incredible turnaround – and their place in the Premier League was confirmed before they even stepped onto the pitch for their next game, as other results went their way. Sunderland were back!

Roy left the players to do most of the celebrating,

but he knew this was an achievement to put alongside some of his best years as a player.

'You all really deserve this,' Roy said while the players jumped and bounced around the dressing room. 'What a year!'

CHAPTER 23

TELLING IT HOW IT IS

Life in the Premier League was tougher – a lot tougher. During the next season, Roy steered Sunderland away from the relegation zone, but then results started to slip and players struggled. He decided it was time for a new voice in the dressing room.

Roy still liked the idea of coaching, though. After a break, he took over briefly as Ipswich manager, but that quickly fell apart.

Still, he was a man in demand, and there was a lot of excitement when Martin O'Neill took over in charge of the Ireland national team in 2013 and named Roy as his assistant manager. Together, they worked hard to improve results, and it felt good to be back around the Irish squad.

Considering that Roy had surprised himself by jumping into the Sunderland role in 2006, he never expected to still be coaching thirteen years later. But by 2019, he was done. He knew he wanted to step away from coaching and spend more time with his family.

Even then, the TV offers came flooding in, and those got Roy's attention. Staying true to himself, he didn't hold back when talking about teams and players – and that's why people loved to listen to him. He was working with Gary and lots of other former players from his generation, and he enjoyed the friendly debates in the comfort of the TV studios.

When he arrived at Old Trafford to give his views on the latest big Premier League game, Roy couldn't help but think back to some of the highlights from his own career. It had been a remarkable journey from Cork to Nottingham to Manchester and the very top of European football, and he was always quick to remind people that his story included a lot of rejection before he finally broke through.

Stepping inside the stadium where he had played so many times also brought him back to the memories of his testimonial game in 2006. Almost 70,000 fans had crowded into Old Trafford that day to pay tribute to Roy's years at the club.

Taking the microphone at the end of the game, he had soaked up the cheers one last time. 'I hope you've had a great night,' he said. 'It's something I'll remember for the rest of my life.'

Roy wasn't sure how much longer he would stay involved in the football world, but he knew he would be walking away with some incredible memories, and a legacy as one of the greatest players to ever wear a Manchester United shirt.

Read on for a sneak preview of
another brilliant football story by
Matt and Tom Oldfield . . .

RONALDO

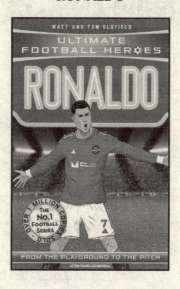

Available now!

CHAPTER 1

EUROPEAN GLORY

Cristiano had already won so many trophies during his amazing career – one Spanish league title, two Spanish cups, three Premier League titles, three English cups, three Champions League trophies and three Ballon d'Ors. But he still felt something was missing. That something was an international trophy with Portugal.

And on 10 July 2016, he was one step away from achieving that dream. With his confidence and goals, Cristiano had led his team all the way to the Euro 2016 final. At the Stade de France, Portugal faced a France team with home advantage and world-class players like Paul Pogba and Antoine Griezmann.

Portugal were the underdogs, but they had the best

player in Europe – Cristiano – and he had never been more determined to win.

After their coach, Fernando Santos, had given his team talk in the dressing room, it was time for the senior players to speak. Nani went first and then it was Cristiano's turn.

'We've done so well to get this far,' their captain told them. 'One more win and we will go down in history. We will return home as heroes!'

The whole squad cheered. Together they could become the champions of Europe.

Cristiano stood with his eyes closed for the Portuguese national anthem. He didn't mumble the words; he shouted them at the top of his voice. He loved his country and he wanted to do them proud on the pitch.

After seven minutes, Cristiano got the ball just inside the French half. As he turned to attack, Dimitri Payet fouled him. The game carried on but Cristiano was still on the ground, holding his left knee and screaming in agony.

Oww!

As the physios used the magic spray and rubbed his knee with an ice pack, Cristiano winced. The injury didn't look good. He put his hands to his face to hide the tears.

Dimitri came over to say sorry for his tackle, but Cristiano was too upset to reply. Eventually, he stood up and limped off the field. On the touchline, he tested his leg – it didn't feel good but he wanted to keep playing.

'Are you sure?' João Mário said to him as he walked back onto the pitch.

'I have to try!' Cristiano told him.

But a minute later, he collapsed to the ground. On his big day, Cristiano was in too much pain to continue. He kept shaking his head – he couldn't believe his bad luck.

'You have to go off,' Nani told him, giving his friend a hug. 'We'll do our skipper proud, I promise!'

Cristiano wasn't ready to give up yet, though. The physios put a bandage around his knee and he went back on again. But when he tried to run, he had to stop. He signalled to the bench: 'I need to come off'.

He ripped off his captain's armband. 'Wear this,' Cristiano said to Nani, putting the armband on him. 'And win this final!'

'Yes, we'll win this for you!' Pepe shouted.

As he was carried off on a stretcher, Cristiano cried and cried. The most important match of his life was over.

It was 0–0 at half-time and Cristiano was there in the dressing room to support his teammates. 'Stick together and keep fighting hard!' he told them.

In the second-half, he was there on the bench, biting his fingernails and, in his head, kicking every ball. Every time Portugal nearly scored, he was up on his feet ready to celebrate. Just before striker Éder went on as a sub, Cristiano looked him in the eyes and said, 'Be strong. You're going to score the winner.'

But after ninety minutes, it was still 0–0. Cristiano walked around giving encouragement to the tired players. It was tough not being out on the pitch, but he could still play his part. After 109 minutes, Éder got the ball, shrugged off the French defender and sent a rocket of a shot into the bottom corner.

Goooooooooooooaaaaaaaaalllllllllllllllllll!!!!!!!!!!!

Cristiano went wild, throwing his arms in the air and jumping up and down. The whole Portugal squad celebrated together. They were so close to victory now.

For the last ten minutes, Cristiano stood with Santos as a second manager. He hobbled along the touchline, shouting instructions to the players.

Run! Defend! Take your time!

At the final whistle, Cristiano let out a howl of happiness as the tears rolled down his cheeks again. He hugged each of his teammates and thanked them.

'No, thank *you!*' Éder said to him. 'Without you, I wouldn't have scored that goal!'

'I told you we'd do it!' Pepe laughed.

Cristiano took his shirt off and threw it into the crowd. They had to give him another one so that he could do his captain's duty – collecting the Euro 2016 trophy.

He climbed the steps slowly, giving high-fives to the fans he passed. The trophy had red and green ribbons, the colours of Portugal's flag. As Cristiano lifted the trophy, the whole team cheered. He kissed it and then passed it on to the other players. No words could describe the joy that Cristiano was feeling.

It was at Manchester United and Real Madrid that he became a superstar, but Cristiano's incredible journey to the top of world football had begun at home in Portugal, with his family, on the island of Madeira. And so the Euro 2016 triumph was a way of saying thanks, for when life wasn't always easy growing up.

Without a difficult start in life, perhaps Cristiano wouldn't have had his amazing hunger to be the best, which turned a special gift into years of glory.

CHAPTER 2

DOLORES AND DINIS

We're going to have another child?' Dolores asked the doctor when he told her the news. She was so shocked that she needed to hear it again. 'Are you sure? I can't believe it!'

Dolores and José Dinis Aveiro already had three children – daughters Elma and Katia, and son Hugo – and it had been eight years since Katia's birth. A fourth child was a real surprise.

'Yes, I'm certain,' the doctor confirmed. 'The news will bring great joy to your house, I'm sure!'

Dolores loved children, but she was worried. Life on the Portuguese island of Madeira was hard. The weather was always good, but many of the people were fed up. A lot of folk were unemployed, especially in the area of Funchal where they lived. The wealthy tourists stayed in the fancy seaside hotels and they never travelled far to spend their money.

Dolores worked hard making wicker baskets to sell, but Dinis had returned from the army and couldn't find a good job. Sometimes, they could only afford to eat bread and soup. And now, they would have another mouth to feed.

'Dinis, what are we going to do?' Dolores said when she got home. She was crying tears of both happiness and sadness.

Space was also a problem. The family lived in the house of Dinis's parents, but there would now be six of them. They didn't have any money to rent a house of their own.

'We'll just have to do the best we can,' Dinis replied.

Dolores agreed. Her fourth child would have a tough start in life but she would do everything possible to make sure they escaped the poverty of Madeira. She was a very strong person and her son or daughter would be too.

When they found out it would be a boy, Dolores's sister suggested the name 'Cristiano' and they liked it. Dolores also chose to call her son after the actor and President of the United States of America, Ronald Reagan.

'It's a good name – the name of an honourable and successful person,' she told her family. Everyone agreed.

Cristiano Ronaldo dos Santos Aveiro.

Cristiano was a big, heavy baby. As the doctor placed him down in a bed, he laughed.

'It's a very good sign,' he said. 'Weighing that much, he could be a footballer!'

Both Dolores and Dinis loved that idea. Dolores was a Sporting Lisbon fan, and her favourite player was their star winger, Luís Figo. Dinis had played football as a young boy and often watched the local team, Andorinha. His friend Fernando Sousa, who would be Cristiano's godfather, was the captain of Andorinha. There were plenty of connections with football.

'Let's hope so!' Dinis replied with a smile.

It wouldn't be easy but anything was possible. They knew that very few youngsters had the special talent to become professional footballers, but it could be the perfect way for their son to leave the poverty of Funchal behind and make a new life somewhere else.

ROY KEANE HONOURS

Nottingham Forest
- FA Cup runners-up, 1991
- League Cup runners-up, 1992

Manchester United
- Premier League winners, 1993–94, 1995–96, 1996–97, 1998–99, 1999–2000, 2000–01, 2002–03
- FA Cup winners, 1993–94, 1995–96, 1998–99, 2003–04
- Champions League winners, 1999
- FA Community Shield, 1993, 1996, 1997, 2003

- 🏆 Intercontinental Cup, 1999
- 🏆 FWA Footballer of the Year, 2000
- 🏆 PFA Players' Player of the Year, 2000

Celtic
- 🏆 Scottish Premier League winners, 2005–06
- 🏆 Scottish League Cup winners, 2005–06

Individual
- 🏆 FAI Young International Player of the Year, 1993, 1994
- 🏆 FAI Senior International Player of the Year, 1997, 2001
- 🏆 FWA Footballer of the Year, 2000
- 🏆 PFA Players' Player of the Year, 2000
- 🏆 Premier League Hall of Fame, 2021

Manager
Sunderland
- 🏆 Championship winners, 2006–07

KEANE

9

THE FACTS

NAME: Roy Maurice Keane

DATE OF BIRTH: 10 August 1971

PLACE OF BIRTH: Cork, Ireland

NATIONALITY: Irish

POSITION: CM

THE STATS

Height (cm):	180
Club appearances:	612
Club goals:	78
Club assists:	45
Club trophies:	20
International appearances:	67
International goals:	9
International trophies:	0
Ballon d'Ors:	0

★ ★ ★ **HERO RATING: 89** ★ ★ ★

GREATEST MOMENTS

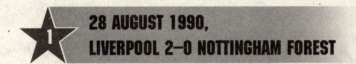
28 AUGUST 1990, LIVERPOOL 2–0 NOTTINGHAM FOREST

In his first full season at Forest, Roy got the stunning news that he was making his debut at Anfield against Liverpool. With his usual mix of crunching tackles and non-stop running, he proved to manager Brian Clough that he belonged on the big stage, even in a loss.

18 AUGUST 1993,
MANCHESTER UTD 3–0 SHEFFIELD UTD

Roy couldn't have dreamed of a better home debut, making himself an instant fan favourite at Old Trafford with two clinical goals. He gave Sheffield United nightmares with his runs from midfield, and it felt great to shake off the pressure of being Britain's most expensive player.

18 JUNE 1994,
IRELAND 1–0 ITALY

There were plenty of ups and downs in Roy's Ireland career, but the famous 1–0 win over Italy at the 1994 World Cup was an unforgettable moment. Battling Roberto Baggio in scorching New York heat, Roy covered every blade of grass to seal the victory.

21 APRIL 1999, JUVENTUS 2–3 MANCHESTER UNITED

On a night of joy and heartbreak for Roy, he led a relentless fightback, turning a 2–0 hole into a 3–2 win, to reach the Champions League final. His header got United back in the game, and he shone brightest in a game packed with stars. The downside? A yellow card that meant Roy would be suspended for the final.

1 FEBRUARY 2005, ARSENAL 2–4 MANCHESTER UNITED

From a fiery showdown with Patrick Vieira in the tunnel to midfield mastery on the pitch, Roy rolled back the years in this thriller at Highbury. United were a team in transition by this point, but this was a reminder of the quality in the squad and of Roy's fearless leadership.

TEST YOUR KNOWLEDGE

QUESTIONS

1. Which English team did Roy support as a boy?

2. What colours did Rockmount AFC wear?

3. Where was Roy when he found out that a Forest scout had been to watch him play?

4. How much did Manchester United pay to sign Roy?

5. Who did Roy and the Irish national team beat 1–0 at the 1994 World Cup?

6. At the start of which season was Roy named United captain?

7. Who did United beat in the 1999 Champions League semi-final?

8. How many Premier League titles did Roy win at United?

9. Who did Roy score his only goal for Celtic against?

10. Which former Ireland teammate contacted Roy about becoming the Sunderland manager?

Answers below . . . No cheating!

1. Tottenham. 2. Yellow and green. 3. In a café. 4. £3.75 million. 5. Italy. 6. 1997–98. 7. Juventus. 8. Seven. 9. Falkirk. 10. Niall Quinn.

PLAY LIKE YOUR HEROES

WIN TACKLES LIKE ROY KEANE

STEP 1: Spot the danger early. You're a box-to-box midfielder and part of the job is understanding when you need to track back and protect the defence. If your team loses the ball, don't waste time waving your arms or slumping your shoulders! Be the first to react.

STEP 2: As the captain, you're a good communicator so let your teammates know where you are. You're sprinting to make the tackle, and they need to know to stay in position and mark the other players.

STEP 3: Decide what kind of tackle is needed. Are you close enough to poke the ball away? Are you going to have to slide to reach it? But think fast! You'll only have a second to make that choice, especially against the speediest players.

STEP 4: Watch the ball and get your timing right. Don't commit too early. If you see the attacker, take a slightly heavy touch – that's your signal to pounce for the tackle. Go in hard but fair – you don't want any yellow or red cards!

STEP 5: What a tackle! Your work doesn't end there, though. Race to the loose ball and pass to a teammate to launch a brilliant counterattack.

CAN'T GET ENOUGH OF
ULTIMATE FOOTBALL HEROES?

Check out heroesfootball.com
for quizzes, games, and competitions!

Plus join the Ultimate Football Heroes
Fan Club to score exclusive content and
be the first to hear about
new books and events.
heroesfootball.com/subscribe/